About the Author

This is my debut book which I wrote at sixteen. When I'm not writing I am most likely playing softball or working out. I am a 2019 All American for softball. I've loved writing from a young age and always knew I wanted to be an author. I decided that age was just a number and why not write a book at sixteen?

Life is for the Living

Grace Dias

Life is for the Living

Olympia Publishers
London

www.olympiapublishers.com
OLYMPIA PAPERBACK EDITION

Copyright © Grace Dias 2024

The right of Grace Dias to be identified as author of
this work has been asserted in accordance with sections 77 and 78 of
the Copyright, Designs and Patents Act 1988.

All Rights Reserved

No reproduction, copy or transmission of this publication
may be made without written permission.
No paragraph of this publication may be reproduced,
copied or transmitted save with the written permission of the publisher,
or in accordance with the provisions
of the Copyright Act 1956 (as amended).

Any person who commits any unauthorised act in relation to
this publication may be liable to criminal
prosecution and civil claims for damage.

A CIP catalogue record for this title is
available from the British Library.

ISBN: 978-1-80439-510-3

This is a work of fiction.
Names, characters, places and incidents originate from the writer's
imagination. Any resemblance to actual persons, living or dead, is
purely coincidental.

First Published in 2024

Olympia Publishers
Tallis House
2 Tallis Street
London
EC4Y 0AB

Printed in Great Britain

Dedication

To my grandpa, for showing me my love for literature and learning. To my mom, the strongest yet kindest person I know. And finally to my dad for always inspiring me to chase those crazy dreams.

Acknowledgements

Thanks to my parents and grandpa once again. I would also like to thank my amazing boyfriend and best friend for proof reading and cheering me on. I would also like to thank all of the amazing trainers at the AP Fresno family for always encouraging me.

Claire, March 2, 2021

It was 3.12 in the morning when my phone went off. I was so groggy I barely knew what was happening. I picked up my phone to what sounded like my mom crying. When I heard the words I'd never thought I'd hear I almost dropped the phone. I felt sick.

"I have to go," I said, my voice breaking as I ran to the bathroom.

The whole way there the words, those dreadful words, just kept repeating in my head. "Cassie is dead." I could hardly breathe. I made it to the bathroom just in time to puke my guts out. I couldn't believe it. My twin sister, my other half, dead. It felt unreal, like I was trapped in some horrible nightmare. I prayed that this was all just some horrible dream and that I would wake up and be able to give my sister a hug. I pinched myself, disappointed to feel it. I went into my parents' room, and sure enough they weren't there.

It all began to really sink in. I would never get to be with my sister ever again in this world. I cried; I cried so hard I started to feel light headed. I thought of all the amazing times I had with my sister, and the amazing memories we had made. It pained me so much to know that it was all gone. No more parties where she forced everyone on the dance floor, no more late night drives with our friends, no more going to the mall or listening to her talk about her soccer matches and baseball games. My sister was the definition of life. She was a huge ball of energy, and she was always positive.

She was the one to always force me and my friends to go out and have fun. She was always the one to do crazy things. She had so many dreams of traveling the world and doing all kinds of crazy stuff like going to spring training, and clubbing in Vegas, and bungee jumping. She was the life of the party.

I guess that's the sad thing about life, you don't realize how much you love it until it's gone.

Harley

I woke up to the sound of my phone going off. *This better be good for someone to call me at 3.47 in the morning*, I thought to myself. I looked at the caller ID and was fairly surprised to see Claire calling at this time. She usually went to bed at like nine. *Maybe it was Cassie using her phone*, I thought. She always stayed up late. I answered the call a little annoyed.

"This better be good for you to be calling at almost four in the morning." I stopped when I heard her try to speak and all that came out was sobs. "Claire, is everything all right?" I heard her pause before finally speaking again.

"Cassie is..." She couldn't even finish the sentence without breaking down.

"Cassie is what? Claire? Claire, what happened to Cassie?" I asked desperately. I started to get scared.

"Cassie is dead," she finally spat out breaking down into tears.

"Claire, this isn't funny! I swear if this is some sort of sick joke—"

"She's gone, Harley. Trust me when I say I really wish that this was some kind of joke," she cut me off.

I couldn't believe it.

"I have to go," I said before I even knew what I was doing. I dropped my phone without realizing out of shock.

I was so sad, mad, confused, and I just felt a whirlwind of emotions, like someone had just hit me with a freight train. But most of all I was mad; I was so mad that someone like Cassie had died. Someone so full of life, that loved every part of it, had hers end so young. It wasn't fair.

Before I had even fully processed what had just happened I threw on a sports bra and shorts and ran downstairs. I got on the treadmill and ran. I ran until my lungs were on fire and my legs were about to give out, then I ran some more. All of my anger boiling inside of me pushing me to keep running, because as long as I kept running it wasn't real. When I ran all that mattered was that I was running. My mind couldn't help but wander to all the memories I had with Cassie.

    I finally stopped the treadmill. When I got off my legs gave out and I didn't fight them. When I finally got to the ground I could feel the hot tears running down my face. All of the breath I had left went to crying.

    Cassie had been my best friend. Out of our friends we were the crazy ones, but she had a nice calm to her that I didn't have. I had a bit of a temper, but she had always been able to calm me down. It wasn't fair. She was such an amazing person. She was a ray of light and she was the one to die. It wasn't fair.

    I had been so overwhelmed that I didn't even ask how she died. My mind went to the worst. I was terrified that someone did this to her. That thought made me even more angry. My anger started to fade into grief the longer I cried.

    Why her?

    I began to cry even harder. I cried until the world slowly started to fade.

Violet

When I heard my phone go off it was 3.57 in the morning. I grabbed my phone and checked the caller ID. When I saw that it was Claire it threw me off a little. Claire loved her beauty sleep.
"Hello," I answered groggily.
"Sorry to wake you." She sounded like she had been crying.
"It's okay. What happened? Is everything okay?" I asked confused.
"No I just…" She stopped to what sounded like stopping herself from breaking down. I began to worry. My mind raced with a thousand different horrible possibilities.
"Claire, I'm your best friend, you can tell me anything." I hoped that she heard the understanding in my voice.
"I know." She took a deep breath before finally speaking. "Cassie died."
"What?" I said as tears filled my eyes.
"I'm sorry I have to go," Claire said before hanging up.
I didn't even fight the tears, I just let them roll down my cheeks. I was a very emotional person, so when I heard that one of my closest friends had died it really drove a dagger through my heart. I was crying so loud that my mom came rushing into my room.
"Violet, what's wrong?" she said with a very worried face.
"She's dead!" I cried.
"Who's dead?"
"Cassie! Cassie is dead!" I sobbed,

As soon as I said it she bombarded me into a hug.

"It's going to be okay, baby." I still felt like crap. I collapsed into her arms and wept and wept while my mom held me like a child. I was in so much pain emotionally that I began to get a headache. Cassie was one of my closest friends. It had always been her, me, Claire, and Harley.

I still remember the day we all met. It was the second week of kindergarten. I met Claire and we became best friends almost immediately, and the same happened with Cassie and Harley. Since Claire and Cassie are twins we all started to hang out and ever since then it's always been the four of us. My ride or dies, but now one of us is gone.

I cried even harder just thinking about it. Cassie was like a sister to me. I don't have any siblings, and my dad died when I was ten so all I had was them and my mom. Now one of them is gone. It's scary because I never thought that I would be losing her anytime soon, but I did, and now I wonder who's next and how soon. That really scared me.

I just wish that I at least got to say goodbye.

Claire

When I woke up the next morning it didn't feel right, like something was missing. I went downstairs to get breakfast. My parents were at the table. No one said a word. It was almost like a thickness hung in the air, almost as if the event last night poisoned the atmosphere.

I poured my cereal and made my coffee in silence. I walked over to the table and managed a few bites. Finally, after eating as much as I could stomach, I got up and went for the door. "I'm going to school now," I called out.

"Okay," my mom said clearly with something else on her mind. She looked exhausted and heartbroken.

It didn't feel right getting into my car without Cassie, especially since she was the one to drive normally. We always picked up Starbucks on Fridays, but it just didn't feel right today. When I got to school it was like the poisonous atmosphere from my house had followed me to school. Rumors had already been spread, and as I walked through the halls everyone whispered as I walked by. A few people even went up to me and told me that they were sorry or that she was too young, and all kinds of other stuff that most of them didn't actually mean.

When I finally made it to my locker Harley and Violet were already there. We didn't say anything for what felt like an eternity as I got my books from my locker. Finally Violet looked at me with her sad, blue eyes and said, "I'm so sorry." It seemed as if she wasn't just apologizing for my hurt.

"It's not your fault," I said my eyes starting to water.

Harley stayed quiet.

"How did she die?" Harley asked while still looking at the ground after what seemed like an eternity of silence.

Violet looked up. It pained me enough to have to tell them that she died, it was gonna be even worse telling how she died.

"She got in a car accident," I said as a few tears started to spill out.

Harley looked at me in a way that showed pain and shock all in one look. "What?" she said, barely able to get it out.

Cassie had loved to drive. She wasn't always a five under the speed limit type of person, but she was always cautious.

"There's also one more thing," I said.

I turned to look at them. I could see the pain written on their faces. Mine probably looked the same

"Brandon was also in the car with her, and he didn't make it out either."

"Who was driving?" Harley asked with a look of fire in her eye.

"I'm pretty sure Cassie was."

"What do you mean, pretty sure? Did you see the aftermath?" Harley asked desperately.

"There is no aftermath."

"How is there no aftermath? They got into a car accident," Harley asked frantically.

I really didn't want to answer that question, but I had to. I looked at Harley who looked like there might be some hope, then I looked at Violet who had stayed quiet this whole time.

She looked at me with pleading eyes that also showed a sign of hope. This was going to suck. "They were driving at night and they ran into an electrical box, which caused the car to explode."

As soon as I said it, I began to cry. Violet was also crying. I looked at Harley, she looked like someone had just stabbed her in the back. Her eyes were watery, but I knew that it took a lot to make Harley cry. I had never seen her cry, but as I looked at her she looked like she was about to break.

"This is bullshit!" she screamed before turning away and storming off to her next class.

Harley

Hearing the way that Cassie died was like a bullet to the foot. I was so mad that my best friend had to die doing something she loved. I was even more mad that the reason that they died was because the car literally exploded. An explosion that not only killed my best friend, but her boyfriend too.

"This is bullshit!" I yelled. I stormed off.

I couldn't stay there. My mind began to play all the memories of Cassie. I remembered the day she got her license. She was so happy. The first thing she did was pick up me, Violet, and Claire and take us to get fast food. We got McDonalds and drove to an empty parking lot and ate in the car while listening to music and talking with each other. I missed that.

I missed that so much my body began to ache. I walked out to the parking lot and got in my car. I drove to McDonalds and ate it in the parking lot. I didn't care if I missed first period, I was too busy missing my best friend.

Violet

The bell rang shortly after Harley ran off. I had no idea where she went, but I was sure that she'd be okay. My first four periods were a blur. I tried my best to pay attention, hoping that it would take my mind off Cassie, but my mind just kept flashing back to memories of her. I was so spaced out I didn't even notice the hand waving in front of me.

"Violet? Violet. VIOLET!" When I came to, I realized that my teacher was standing in front of me and my class was empty.

"I'm so sorry," I said scrambling to get up and collect all of my things.

"It's okay, Violet. Just so you know the bell rang about three minutes ago. I was about to call the nurse's office. I do hope that you were paying attention for at least a little bit of class."

"I'm sorry I just have a lot on my mind."

"Just please pay attention next time. I'll let this one go since you're a good kid," my teacher said, giving me a sympathetic smile.

I returned the smile.

"Thank you, Mr. S, I promise that it won't happen again."

"I will hold you to that. Have a good day, Violet."

"You too," I called walking out of class.

Thank God I was such a good student. If I didn't have straight As including my four AP classes I don't think I could've gotten out of that so easily. When I got to my lunch spot Claire and Harley were both there. I was a little bit surprised that Harley was back. As soon as I sat down I remembered why today sucked almost immediately. No matter how much I tried to shake it, it just felt like something was missing.

Claire

After Harley left this morning I felt even worse. I didn't even bother paying attention in first period, or any of the first four for that matter. When I got to lunch Harley was already at our spot. "Where did you go?" I asked.

"McDonalds," she answered as if it was the most casual thing in the world.

She didn't look at me. Her gaze was at the sky. She seemed to have a bit on her mind. "Cassie loved that place," I said, sitting down next to her.

I joined her in looking at the sky. I saw her face in every cloud. "That's why I went. Plus I wanted fries." That made me smile. It was the first time I smiled all day.

"Did you at least bring the rest of us any?" I asked with a smile.

"Hey, get your own fries," she said smiling.

I'm pretty sure that that was her first smile of the day too.

"Cassie would have made you drive back there to get the rest of us fries," I pointed out.

"I know," she said.

Our smiles faded after that. After a few minutes we both turned our heads to see Violet walking up.

"What took you so long?" I asked.

"I spaced out in class and didn't realize until a few minutes after the bell, and if you were wondering, the only reason I realized was because Mr. S had to yell my name for apparently long enough to worry him," Violet explained, looking frazzled.

She was by no means a rule breaker.

"Violet, dozing off in class?" Harley said with a fake gasp. "Do your parents know, young lady?" That got a smile out of all three of us.

"And how many periods did you skip over there Ms. goody-2-shoes?" Violet said laughing.

"Only one, which was chemistry, and last time I checked I'm literally never going to use that stuff in real life." We all started laughing for about a minute.

It didn't last very long. We just sat there in silence after, all with the same thing on our minds. I looked back up at the sky. I sat, looking at the Cassie-looking clouds, and wondered if she really was watching me.

Harley

After my little McDonalds... "Adventure" I went back to school. I went back right before second period. I didn't listen to one of my teachers, but at least I was there. I was the first one to our lunch spot, which is rare.

After Claire and Violet got there we actually smiled and laughed for about a minute. For a whole minute it was as if nothing happened, as if it were a normal day and Cassie would show up any minute and say something to make us laugh even harder, but she didn't. All three of us must've realized it at the same time because we all stopped laughing.

I looked back up at the sky.

We sat there in silence for what must've been five minutes before, without even realizing it, I spoke.

"I really miss her." I hadn't even realized I even said it out loud for a second.

"I think we all do," Claire said, also looking at the sky.

The rest of lunch was mostly silence with a bit of small talk here and there. We all knew what all three of us were thinking. I didn't say any of it out loud because the more I talked about it the more real it was, and if I had to guess, Claire and Violet didn't bring it up for the same reason.

It didn't help that Claire looked just like Cassie both with straight light brown hair with little touches of gold and red. The main difference was their build and eyes. Claire was just skinny while Cassie was also skinny but toned from soccer. Their eyes are what really separated them though, Claire had hazel eyes, while Cassie had amber eyes. Cassie's eyes looked light brown most of the time but when they hit the light they had little flakes of gold in them.

After lunch I didn't even look at the board in my last two classes, not that it was different from any other day.

After school, as I walked to the locker room, I already knew that this was going to be a tough practice. Me and Cassie have been playing soccer together since first grade.

When I got out of the locker room I was bombarded with hugs and apologies and offers to talk from my teammates. I could tell that they were grieving too, well most of them. The one girl who didn't come up to me was Amanda. She and Cassie never got along. They played the same position and she was always Cassie's backup.

Practice actually went a lot better than I expected. The running and drills kept me distracted. After practice I walked over to the supply closet to put some equipment away when I heard a voice that sounded like Amanda's coming from inside.

"Honestly I think everyone is making a huge deal out of it."

"I mean she did die," said what sounded like one of the freshmen, who sounded very annoyed.

"Yeah I know but it shouldn't have to bring the entire team down. It's not like no one else can play that position," Amanda shot back, annoyed.

"Amanda, that's pretty messed up." The freshman sounded horrified.

"I'm not saying I'm happy she died or anything, I'm just saying Karma's a bitch."

I was so mad I was shaking. Before I even knew what was

happening I dropped the equipment and stormed inside the closet. When I got in there Amanda looked like she saw a ghost.

"Since Karma is such a bitch I hate to see what it has in store for you," I hissed.

"It's not my fault she died," she scoffed.

That was the last straw.

I punched her. I punched her hard. She fell back and I practically tackled her. I started punching and didn't stop. I used all of my anger and sadness to fuel me. After I got a few hits in I felt someone pull me off. The freshman must have gotten Coach. He was not happy. When Amanda got up it looked like she had a broken nose. I guess Karma really was a bitch.

"HARLEY!" my coach screamed, pulling me off her. "What the fuck was that?" my coach roared as I stood up.

Oh shit, I thought.

So practice did end up being tough after all. After getting yelled at by my coach and having to do suicides as a punishment I finally got home.

I didn't sleep well that night. Images of what happened earlier and Cassie kept my mind up all night. The next morning seemed to go by in slow motion. I skipped fourth period, the period before lunch. I went to pick up McDonalds, and this time I got enough for all three of us. I was the last one to our spot today.

"Did you get enough for all of us this time?" Claire asked as if she didn't already know the answer.

"Depends on how nice you are today," I answered handing her a cheeseburger.

We actually smiled and laughed at that lunch. I wondered if Cassie was watching down on us right now. It was so unfair that she had to go so young. There was so much stuff that she wanted to do.

She made this bucket list when she was thirteen of all the things she wanted to do before she died. There was a bunch of awesome stuff on there like bungee jumping, and partying in Vegas; it's so unfair that she didn't get to do one thing. That's when it hit me. I realized a way that we could almost make it to where Cassie was with us.

"I got it!" I yelled. Claire and Violet stopped and looked up at me confused.

"Got what?" Claire asked.

"Are you feeling okay?" Violet asked, looking concerned.

"I'm fine, great actually." They looked at each other concerned then back at me. "I know what we can do for Cassie." Both of their eyes widened. "Do you remember her bucket list?" I asked.

"Yeah," they answered in unison.

Claire raised an eyebrow.

"What if we do it for her? To honor her, to live like she would've wanted us to, live like she wanted to. It'll be our way of almost letting her live through us. We don't have to do everything on it, but we can get through a good chunk of it."

Violet

When Harley walked up she looked so sad, but then the more we all talked and laughed, the less and less sad she looked. When she said her idea I didn't think that I could say yes, especially when I knew that my mom would most likely say no anyway considering that Cassie's bucket list included partying in Vegas and visiting three different states, and a foreign country, but when I looked at Harley and how hopeful she looked I couldn't help but say, "Sounds awesome."

I felt horrible for giving her what was most likely false hope, but a part of me still had hope. I knew it probably didn't count for anything, but sometimes hope is all we have.

Claire

I was about to say no to Harley, but when Violet agreed it made me think of my sister and how happy she was when she made the bucket list. She read the whole thing to me with such enthusiasm. I know that if she were here she would tell me, *Screw it, if you want to do it then do it. I mean you have to have something to tell your future kids after all.* I could practically hear her voice.

I looked up at Violet and Harley. "I'm in," I said.

When I got home I was shaking just thinking about asking my mom. I really believed that she was going to say no, which is why I kept putting it off, because the longer I put it off the more real it seemed. When I finally got up the courage to ask, I went downstairs. She was sitting at the table looking at baby photos of me and Cassie.

"Hey, could I talk to you?" I asked shakily.

She looked up and smiled a soft smile at me. "Of course, baby." She looked drained.

It was easy to tell she had been crying. Our kitchen table was covered in pictures of Cassie. "That's a good one," I said, picking up a picture of Cassie and me.

We were eight and both had on star sunglasses with dresses and our mom's heels. I smiled down at the picture.

"Everything okay?" I looked up at the sound of her soft voice.

"Yeah." I put the picture down. "Do you remember Cassie's bucket list?" I asked. She looked up and thought for a minute.

"Yes, I think so."

"Well, I know it's a lot to ask but me, Harley, and Violet wanna go do it for her. We'll skip the partying stuff and super dangerous stuff, but we really wanna do this. We want to do it for Cassie." She looked like she was about to say no, but stopped herself.

She looked at the picture I had set down, mainly at Cassie then back at me. She took a deep breath. She looked back up at me. She looked at me for a moment. She looked older than before, as if the past two days aged her.

"Fine but only if you skip the partying and super dangerous stuff, and you call me every night." I got up and hugged her before she could finish.

"Thank you so much, I promise to call you every night."

"I love you so much," she said squeezing me.

I gave her a good squeeze back.

"I love you too," I said before letting go.

I ran upstairs and called Violet and Harley and told them I could go. Harley's parents had said yes too, which was not that surprising, so all we were waiting on was Violet's mom.

I thought back to back to my mom after I got back. She looked so sad, and my dad was practically on autopilot. Losing Cassie had really taken a hit on them.

I went back downstairs to find my mom on the couch. She was watching old home videos of me and Cassie. My dad was sitting next to her. I didn't say anything, I just walked over and sat down next to my mom. I put my head on her shoulder. She was also silent. She kissed the top of my head, and rested her head on top of mine.

We sat there silent, watching the missing part of our family.

Violet

I was a little bit shocked to hear that Claire's mom had said yes. She had always been so strict with her and Cassie, maybe her death had an even bigger effect than we thought.

When my mom got home from work I had just finished making dinner. I tried to make dinner most nights since my mom worked so hard. She was a lawyer and a single mom so she already had enough on her plate, so I figured that making dinner was the last thing she wanted to do, even if she never said it out loud.

"It looks amazing, Vi," she said sitting down after she got a plate. I sat down across from her with a plate of my own.

"Thanks." I hesitated for a minute before continuing, "Do you mind if I ask you something?" My mom looked up. She grabbed my hands from across the table and gave them a little squeeze.

"You can ask me anything, darling," she said sweetly. I smiled at her.

"Well Cassie had this bucket list and Harley and Claire and I wanted to do it for Cassie. Both of their parents said yes. I know it's asking for a lot but it would really mean a lot to me, and I'll get all of my school work done ahead of time."

"And Claire's mom said yes?" she asked, surprised.

"Yes." She thought about it for a moment and then looked at me.

"You are an amazing kid, and if Claire's mom said yes then

it must not be that bad, so you can go."

I was shocked. I was actually going to be able to go. "Thank you!" I squealed while hugging her.

After dinner I called Claire and Harley. "She said yes!" I exclaimed into the phone.

"Wait, so this is actually happening?" Claire asked.

"Hell yeah it is!" Harley said.

I couldn't believe it, we were going to do this. We were going to complete Cassie's bucket list. We were going to live for the dead.

Harley

Don't get me wrong, I knew that when I told Claire and Violet my crazy idea it was a long shot, but I had hope, it wasn't much; but this little sliver of hope that I would be able to almost say goodbye without saying goodbye.

When I heard that both of their parents said yes I was ecstatic. I knew that my parents would say yes. Both of my parents were surgeons, so they were at work a lot. They thought that letting me be with my friends as long as I was safe was better than having me be alone all the time.

Don't get me wrong I was super grateful for my life, and I know that my parents loved me to shreds, but I just wish I got a little more time with them. I guess that one of the reasons I was so close with my friends, when I wasn't at soccer practice, which I played with Cassie, I was at one of their houses which caused the other two to come. In a way we were one big family.

I went upstairs to call and actually plan the trip out, well Claire called to plan it out. "Heyyyyy," I said.

"Hi. So are you ready to plan?" Claire asked.

"Duh," I said as if it wasn't even a question.

"Okay so I found her bucket list under her bed. One of the things on here says to travel to three different states, and one new country. I was thinking that we would fly out to Vegas, then drive to LA in Cali, then drive to Arizona, then fly to Mexico and fly home from there. I figured that we just do one flight straight to Mexico since it's the farthest from Ohio."

"That's perfect!" I said excitedly. I was so ready for this trip.

"I'm not even done yet." She laughed. "We can do all the crazy things on her bucket list while we're over there, which you can be in charge of planning," she finished.

"Awesome."

I had no idea how I was supposed to wait more than five minutes for this trip. "That's a yes I assume?" Claire asked with a laugh.

"Duh," I said once again.

"Okay, cool. I'll call Violet and fill her in."

"All right, bye," I said.

"Bye," Claire said, hanging up. This wait was going to be torture.

Violet

I was super excited when Claire called and told me the plan. I could hardly sleep that night, I was so excited. The next morning school seemed to go by in slow motion, but I was able to pay attention this time. The last thing I needed was another lecture.

At lunch we met at our spot as usual. I was the first one there. When Claire and Harley walked up they looked just as excited as I did.

"You wanna go get Taco Bell?" Harley asked. "I'm going no matter what, but I would appreciate some company."

"Umm I'm not missing out on Taco Bell," Claire stated with a smile on her face.

"Sounds fun," I replied.

We walked to the car smiling and laughing as usual thinking about the trip.

When we got to the parking lot we made sure no one was looking then sank into Harley's car. It was a Mustang convertible. The rule at our school was that only seniors were allowed to go off campus for lunch, but we snuck past the teachers anyway. We usually only did this about three times a week, plus we were already juniors, so it wasn't horrible.

As soon as we were a good distance from the school Harley started blasting music that we all sang along to off key. That's when I started to think back to Cassie.

We usually took her car; Harley would sit up front with her, and me and Claire would sit in the back. It felt weird without her.

The one time we did get caught she was able to talk her way right out of it and get away with only a warning. She always knew just what to say.

We pulled up to Taco Bell about ten minutes after we left school. Once we got our food and sat down we began to talk about the trip.

"Okay so what are we wearing?" I asked.

"Super skimpy bikinis, duh," Harley said, rolling her eyes.

Claire and I laughed as Harley playfully smacked her on the arm.

"We are going to Mexico after all, we might as well embrace it." Harley laughed.

"My mom would kill me," Claire said.

"Me too," I chimed in.

"She never killed Cassie," Harley pointed out. Cassie did love her… Non-motherly clothes.

"Cassie was also a much better liar than me," Claire countered.

"Come on, you can't let me be the only person in one," Harley whined.

"Then just wear a one piece," I suggested.

Harley rolled her eyes.

"But you get way hotter guys in a bikini," she said, smiling. Claire smiled and rolled her eyes.

"Okay fine, but only in Mexico," Claire said, finally giving in.

"Deal," Harley quickly replied.

We all laughed. Then it got quiet. It was almost as if we were all struck with the exact same thought.

"Cassie did love her bikinis," I said.

"I think she loved them a little too much even though they

were a little too little," Claire said, starting to smile a little.

"Least I had someone to make me look like a good influence," Harley said smiling.

That made me laugh for a minute, then the silence fell over us again. Harley looked up at Claire with sad eyes.

"When's the funeral?" she asked.

"Tomorrow," Claire said without looking up.

We drove back to school after that. The ride back was silent with no music.

Claire

After getting back to school I was still a little sad, but it was slowly getting better over time. I paid a little more attention in class today and actually did my homework. The next day was the hardest.

It was the day of Cassie's funeral. It was a Saturday so we didn't have to miss school along with a handful of people from our school. Some were just there for show, while others were there to actually say goodbye. The school had been kind to me and my family. They put a poster of Cassie over the staircase.

Harley and Violet met at my house before so we could go together. When they walked inside we all exchanged hugs with each other and our parents. We went upstairs while their parents went into the living room to talk. When we got upstairs I was about to open the door to my room when I realized that I hadn't been in Cassie's room since she died except for when I got the bucket list. I took the hand off the knob and went across the hall. I looked at Harley and Violet before I opened the door.

"I haven't been in there since she died except when I looked for the bucket list," I said looking down.

Before either of them could respond I turned around and opened the door and walked inside with Harley and Violet trailing around me.

The room was the same as always. Band posters on the wall, a messy unmade bed with clothes on the floor and bed, a record player with vinyls in the corner, and the shirtless Cole Sprouse poster hanging on the ceiling above her bed.

"It feels like nothing changed," Harley said, almost taking the words right out of my mouth.

I smiled, we always hung out in her room. We used to have a boardgame night every Thursday in summer. It was Cassie's idea, she said that Thursday was like Friday Eve and just needed that little extra push to make it feel like we had two Fridays, especially since we didn't have school in summer.

"Stay here," I said.

I went to our game closet and got Uno out, it was our favorite game. I walked back into the room as soon as I got it.

"We have time for one round," I said holding the pack of cards out.

Harley

When I woke up this morning all I could think about was the funeral. I dreaded it. When I got to Claire's we ended up in Cassie's room. Claire brought in Uno. It reminded me of Summer game night. Uno was always fun, especially since I always won. I, as usual, continued my winning streak.

When we walked downstairs to leave I started to remember why I was dreading this. I felt like this was truly saying goodbye. We all got in Claire's car that used to be Cassie's and drove to the service. I ended up driving. Since Cassie passed I became the designated driver.

We got there early so we could set up. There were a lot of people that showed up. Some of them didn't even care about Cassie; they were popular and just using it to get attention for themselves. It made me so angry. I was about to go over and yell at them when I saw Brandon's family walk by.

I had been so caught up in Cassie's death that I forgot that Brandon had also died. Brandon and Cassie had been together for two years. I had been to Brandon's house a few times; Cassie would try to set me up with one of Brandon's friends. I never had the heart to flat out tell her that I wasn't really a commitment type of person, but I'm pretty sure she figured it out anyway. It's not that I didn't like any of his friends, or any of the other guys I've dated for that matter, but I just never really took it seriously. The longest relationship I've had was three months. I guess that if I actually liked the guy I just didn't want the stress of it.

When Brandon's mom saw me she smiled and walked over. "Hi, Ms. Rebrio." I said smiling as she walked over.

"Hello, dear, but I told you, you can just call me Susan," she said smiling.

"Okay, Susan," I said.

She smiled, and then looked at me with sympathy in her eyes. She knew how close me and Cassie were.

"How have you been holding up?" she asked.

"I've been okay," I said, holding a fake smile.

She nodded then gave me a smile and took my hand. I didn't feel right complaining when she lost someone too.

"You're a very strong young lady." She looked sympathetic. I smiled for real.

"Thank you. So what about you?" I asked.

I wish that she didn't also have to go through this.

"I've also been okay, but I would also be lying if I said it wasn't hard, he was my baby boy after all." There was a sadness in her eyes as she spoke about it.

"I'm so sorry, I can only imagine," I said, taking her hand.

"Don't be, you lost your best friend, that's not exactly easy either."

"That means a lot." She smiled and gave my hand a light squeeze.

"Sometimes life takes us by surprise doesn't it?"

"No kidding," I agreed.

That got a small laugh from her.

I told her about the bucket list and how everyone else was holding up, and she told me how her husband and the boys, her two other sons, were doing. Finally she looked up and must have seen Claire's mom.

"It's been nice talking to you, Harley. I'm going to go talk to Lori," she said, showing a sweet smile.

"It was nice talking to you too, and I hope it gets easier."

"The same to you."

She smiled and gave my hand one last squeeze before letting go and finally walking away. I could see why Cassie loved her so much.

Claire

The funeral was tough at first, especially setting up. I felt horrible having to hang up pictures of my dead sister. It got better as it went on though. It made me happy to see Harley talk with Ms. Rebrio, she had been like a second mom to Harley.

Claire used to drag Harley on double dates and they would usually meet at Brandon's house. I felt bad not telling Cassie that Harley wasn't exactly the stable relationship type of gal, but I'm pretty sure she already knew. If Harley wanted to, she could easily get a long term boyfriend. She was in great shape from soccer, decently tall at about five foot six, and had long straight dark black hair with deep blue eyes, and bright skin with little to no acne.

She was very pretty and could easily get a boyfriend with her personality, but she just doesn't like commitment, meanwhile me and Violet were just awkward and got nervous around boys. Violet was also very pretty with wavy bleach blond hair, about five foot four, and a tiny waist. The problem with Violet is that she's naturally quiet and can't tell when a guy is into her even when it is very obvious. I'm just straight up awkward, I never know what to say to guys.

Cassie tried to give me pointers, but it was no use. Cassie knew how to date though. She had a few boyfriends before Brandon, but they never really lasted; she got her heart broken, and broke a few herself, but she really loved Brandon.

It scared me at first, and I wondered if they fell in love too fast, but it was hard to argue that after seeing them together. He was her world, and she was his. They loved each other more than anything in this world. Maybe they were meant to die together, because it would be more painful for one to live without the other.

Violet

The funeral sucked. It was so hard having to, in a way, say goodbye. It felt like a fake goodbye, like it was already too late. I wish I was able to say goodbye for real.

I saw Ms. Rebrio talk to Harley. That helped put a smile on my face. I know that Harley's parents are a bit distant, and that Ms. Rebrio is like a mom to her. Cassie also loved Ms. Rebrio. They would always joke about her and Brandon's future wedding and children.

Sometimes I feel like part of it, like the bridesmaids' dresses weren't a total joke. When it was time for speeches, Harley, Claire and I each gave a speech. I almost broke down in the middle of my speech. It was so hard for me to go up there and talk about my dead friend when I knew that I would never see her again. I was thankfully able to get through the speech without completely breaking down.

The drive back to Claire's was quiet, without music or small talk. We were all thinking about her. When we got back to Claire's we said our goodbyes and went home.

I could hardly sleep that night, my brain was full of memories, and excitement for the future. I tossed and turned through the night. We plan to leave in a week for our trip. I couldn't wait to finally say goodbye truly. I just wished that she could go with us.

Harley

The next week was a blur, but somehow I actually somewhat paid attention in my classes. I had tons of homework since I was doing it in advance, but it was worth it. Before I knew it was the night before we left. I was packing when I decided to call Claire.

"Hello," she answered.

"Hey. Quick question, which color do you want, light blue, dark blue, or light purple?"

"Why?" she asked skeptically.

"I got us matching bikinis," I said casually.

"Will they cover my butt?" Her skepticism still present.

"Define cover." I tried my best to glide around the question.

"I'll take that as a no," she assumed.

She was technically right.

"Okay hear me out, they're super cute," I pleaded.

"Fine." She sighed, but I could hear a smile in her voice.

"So what color will it be?" I asked.

"Light blue."

"Perfect," I said, making a mental note.

"I better go now."

"Okay bye," I said, hanging up. I called Violet next.

"Quick Question," I said. "What color do you want, light purple or dark blue?"

"What for?" she asked curiously.

I knew I would have to sell her on this.

"I got us matching bikinis," I said, trying to stay casual.

"I told you I'm not wearing one," she whined.

"We both knew that was a lie as soon as you said it."

"Fine but only because you're my friend."

"You won't regret it," I promised, even though she probably would.

"I sure hope not. I'll take light purple."

"Okay, I'll let you pack now."

"Okay, bye."

After I hung up I finished packing. I couldn't sleep that night, I was so full of excitement, but a part of me still felt like something was missing. Cassie would be so excited if she were here, she would make sure everyone did crazy and fun things.

I got up and threw on a sports bra and shorts and hopped on the treadmill. I loved to run, it gave me the time to think or just ignore everything. I thought about Cassie and how many crazy things we did together before she died. I decided to promise myself something at that moment, I promised myself that I would make sure that all three of us have the time of our lives on our trip. I ran for a bit longer then finally decided that my body had enough. I hopped off and checked the time, it was 2.17 in the morning. We had an eight o'clock flight in the morning which meant that I had to wake up at around five. Only three more hours to go.

Claire

The last past week was crazy with packing, school, and managing the excitement for the trip. Throughout the past week I felt at war with myself, part of me was super excited for the trip, while the other felt it unfair that Cassie couldn't be here. She would've been calling Harley every night leading up to the trip talking about how excited she was, and picking out outfits, which would eventually end up on the floor of her bedroom.

The night before we left I was up tossing and turning all night. I got up and went into Cassie's room. I looked up at the Cole Sprouse poster and smiled. I remember when she first got it; it was a birthday gift from Harley. My dad still has no idea it exists.

I stood in the room that was once so familiar and took a deep breath letting all of the memories sink in. I thought back to all four of us in here with facemasks, watching cheesy movies and eating junk food. I walked out and went back to bed.

When I got up it was an hour before we had to leave. Shortly after I finished getting ready I took my luggage downstairs right as the doorbell rang. Violet was the first to arrive, as usual, with her mom; Harley came not too long after. Violet looked full of energy ready to get on the plane, while Harley on the other hand stood with her hair in a messy bun and a Starbucks drink in hand. She was never much of a morning person.

"There weren't any later flights?" Harley complained.

"You said that you wanted to get there ASAP, remember." I

smiled.

"Yeah, I was talking about day wise." She groaned.

"Don't worry you can sleep on the plane." I laughed.

We loaded our luggage into my mom's car. I went back into my house to say goodbye to my dad.

"We're leaving now, just thought I'd say goodbye," I said as I walked in the living room. He looked up from the newspaper and smiled.

"I'm gonna miss you, kid," he said. I smiled. "I'm so proud of you. I know it's been hard without Cassie, but I am so grateful that I still have one of my beautiful daughters," he said, getting up to hug me. "Go have fun out there, the world is such a beautiful place."

"I will, Cassie would have wanted it that way," I said with my head in his chest.

Violet

When I got up that morning it was the day we were leaving. I woke up before my mom and made us some breakfast. Once I finished cooking I got ready and went back into the kitchen to see that my mom had plated the food and waited for me before she started eating.

"Are you excited?" She beamed.

"I can't wait," I said in between bites.

I was so excited, I had always wanted to see more than Ohio. "I'm so happy for you, but make sure you stay safe."

"I promise I will," I assured her.

She reached across the table and squeezed my hand. I was gonna miss her. "I texted some easy dinner recipes for when I'm gone," I said.

She gave me a small smile.

"That's sweet, but I think I'll just be ordering takeout," she said smiling. I laughed. She had never been much of a cook.

After breakfast we put my luggage in the car and went to Claire's. While Claire said goodbye to her dad, I did the same with my mom, and Harley with her parents. After our goodbyes Claire's mom drove us to the airport. After going through security and checking in we finally arrived at our gate.

"I'm gonna go get another coffee, do you guys want anything?" Harley said, still looking drained.

"I'm okay," I said.

"No thanks," said Claire.

"All right, I'll be right back," Harley said over her shoulder while leaving.

Claire looked at me and smiled. "What?" I asked.

"Did you ever think that we would be a part of something this crazy?" she said, almost amazed. That made me laugh a little.

"Nope, this sounds more like a Cassie and Harley adventure," I agreed.

It really did feel unreal. Me and Claire were never risk takers. We both usually stuck to rules. "Definitely. You know what. Let's live this trip. Let's be crazy this trip," Claire said, looking like it was just a thought said out loud.

I looked at her; her eyes were filled with hope. "Let's do it," I agreed.

Harley

I couldn't believe that we were actually at the airport about to actually do this. If I'm being totally honest, when I told Claire and Violet about this idea, I was about ninety-seven percent sure that it wasn't going to happen, but it did. It's almost as if the universe wanted this to happen.

The funny thing about life is you don't realize how much you love someone or something until it's gone. I missed my best friend so much, but I had to be grateful for the people that are still in my life right now. I was so grateful for Claire and Violet, they were like sisters to me.

After I got my coffee I went back to our gate just in time to board. We were at the back of the plane so we had to wait a little bit to board. The plane was huge.

There were ten seats in a row, three on one side, a walkway, four in the middle, a walkway, and three on the other side. We were on the right side of the plane. I took the window seat with Claire in the middle, and Violet on the aisle seat.

"Okay, what movie are we watching?" I asked, as we sat down.

"Horror," Claire said.

"Umm, no thank you, how about romance?" Violet suggested.

"Comedy it is," I said.

We all laughed. Whenever we couldn't agree on a movie we would just put on a comedy since everyone liked them. The flight took about four hours, so just enough time for two short movies.

During the second movie we were too busy talking to pay attention. "I can't believe we're going to Vegas!" Violet squealed.

"Me either, you think my fake ID looks legit?" I asked pulling it out. Claire rolled her eyes while Violet giggled.

"You did not," Claire said sarcastically.

"Oh, but I did," I said smiling. "Don't worry, I got you guys some too," I said, pulling them out of my backpack.

"Taking you to Vegas is a horrible idea," Claire said.

"You may be right, but it's a pretty fun one," I said.

Claire smiled while rolling her eyes. We landed not too long after that. We ordered an Uber and went outside. Once we were in the car we all sat down.

"Where to?" the driver asked.

"The Neon Boneyard please," I said.

"Yes, mam," he said starting the car. I looked at Claire and Violet.

"Okay, so I thought we could go to the Neon Boneyard first, since that's on the bucket list, and then we could go to the hotel when it gets dark. It's the only activity not on the strip. I figured we'd do that first," I explained.

"Sounds like a plan," Claire said.

Claire

The Neon Boneyard was like nothing I've ever seen before. It was filled with all of the old neon signs in Vegas, it was totally awesome. It was about nine forty-five when we got there, but I was still used to Ohio time, which was twelve forty-five.

We spent pretty much the whole day there. Once it started to get dark we decided to head to our hotel, which was Caesars.

"That was so awesome!" Violet squealed, getting in the Uber, which was this cool convertible.

"Hell yeah it was!" Harley agreed.

"What a great way to start off the trip," I cooed.

I could see why my sister had wanted to go there so bad.

We laughed and talked until we got to the strip. Once we were in eyesight of the strip I looked up and lost my breath. I had heard how beautiful it was at night, but it was such a sight. We were in heavy traffic so I stood up and stared in awe. Harley must've felt the same because she also got up along with Violet. It was truly pulchritudinous. The strip's beauty literally took my breath away. I felt like I was on another planet.

"First time in Vegas?" our Uber driver asked, laughing to himself.

"Is it that obvious?" I said with an awkward laugh.

"Not to be a buzzkill but traffic is about to start up again and I wouldn't want any of you flying out of the car," he said, with a smile.

I nodded and all three of us quickly sat back down.

The rest of the ride all three of us looked at all of the different sights. I couldn't help but stare in awe at all of the different lights and sights.

When we finally got to the hotel we took our luggage out of the trunk.

"Have a nice night, ladies. I hope you enjoy more than the lights," the driver said driving off.

"Thank you," I called out as he drove off.

Our hotel was huge. The lobby was a circle shape with a Greek statue in the middle, and marble floors and walls. Our room was like any other, with a queen bed and a pull out, but there was one thing that made it different, our balcony. The balcony looked over the fountain in the middle of Caesars. It was beautiful.

I was standing on the balcony admiring the view when my stomach started to growl. I walked back inside the room.

"You guys ready for dinner?" I said.

"Sounds good to me," Harley started. "There is a giant mall under our hotel," she said with a grin.

"Then let's go," I said with a smile.

My stomach let out another growl. I looked at Harley as she looked at me. After a moment we both burst into laughter.

Violet

Las Vegas was absolutely stunning, even the lobby of our hotel was a grand sight. After getting lost a few times, we were able to successfully navigate our way to the mall. The mall was massive with tons of stores, restaurants, and even an art gallery. It was almost as if you were actually in ancient Greece, set underground with white pillars along the wall, and statues of Greek gods, but the most peculiar thing to me was the "sky".

The "sky" was just very detailed art to look like it was always day. It was a bit mesmerizing in a way. I couldn't help but stare at it as we walked by.

We finally settled to eat at the Cheesecake Factory after walking around a bit. As we were sitting down I couldn't help but think about how much more fun this would be if Cassie were here, but then I remembered the promise that me and Claire made in the airport.

If Cassie could tell us something somehow, she would tell all three of us to have the time of our lives. I almost always ordered from the skinny menu from here, but I decided that I deserved a bomb meal, that's what Cassie would have wanted. The server came by to take our drink order, we all got Shirley Temples. When the server came back to take our order I let Claire and Harley order first.

"I'll have a grilled cheese and tomato soup please," I said confidently. I sat up straight when I ordered it. I know it isn't exactly "rebellious" but I was not a very rebellious person. I couldn't remember the last time I got lower than an A on a test, or had to be asked to do my chores.

"Your orders will be right up," our server said, as he finished up writing on his little notepad. Claire looked at me with an eyebrow raised.

"You graduated from the skinny menu?" she asked, her eyebrow still raised. I shrugged.

"I decided that I deserved a grilled cheese," I said, smiling proudly.

"Good for you, Vi." Claire beamed.

"Good thing you did, healthy food is ass," Harley said. We all giggled, and Claire rolled her eyes.

"After this we have to go shopping," I said, changing the subject from my boldness.

"Umm why do you think that we decided to stay in a place with an underground mall?" Harley said smiling, as if it were the most obvious thing in the world.

I smiled.

I couldn't help but feel truly happy in this moment, with my two best friends, sitting in the Cheesecake Factory in Caesars Palace in Las Vegas. I felt so lucky to have these two girls with me, it was sad that Cassie couldn't be here, but when she died I started to realize that you have to cherish moments like these, where you can feel truly happy, or when you are surrounded by the people you love, because nothing lasts forever.

I know that this vacation isn't going to last forever, so my goal is to enjoy every last bit of it, and hopefully get some closure about Cassie. I looked at Harley, who seemed to be lost in her own thoughts.

"Cassie would have really loved this place," Harley finally said, with an almost sad smile.

"Isn't that why we're here, to live for her?" I said.

Claire smiled sympathetically at me.

"Of course," Claire said. "My sister is probably smiling down on us right now." I returned the smile.

Harley

I had only been in Las Vegas for less than a day, but that's all it took for me to fall in love. When we first drove through the strip I couldn't help but picture Cassie sitting next to me staring at all the lights. I really wished she were here. If she were here she would be dragging Claire and Violet to the clubs; but she wasn't here so it was my job, after shopping of course.

Dinner was fantastic, I could already see Violet letting loose just a little bit, even if it was in her own way. After we finished our dinner we decided to share a slice of cheesecake.

"To Cassie," I said, raising my fork.

"To Cassie," Claire and Violet echoed, toasting their forks with mine.

The cheesecake was, as expected, incredible. After we paid we went out to go shopping. While walking around we bumped into a giant H&M. I didn't even have to look behind me to know that Claire and Violet were also walking towards the store. We stopped at a display with a bunch of party dresses. "All right we all have to get one," I said.

"Way ahead of you," Claire said, digging through the racks of dresses.

Violet giggled a little bit then joined Claire on digging through dresses. I decided that I should start looking too. Violet finally picked out a baby soft pink dress with a deep v neck, spaghetti straps, and that also happened to be really sparkly. I decided on a navy long sleeve dress, that also had a deep v neck, but had a slit for my midriff, which was a perfect amount of tightness on my body, and of course the dress happened to be very sparkly. Claire, who took her dear sweet time, finally picked a white dress with spaghetti straps, which was tight on the top and flowy on the bottom, which was also very sparkly.

I think Vegas has a thing for sparkly.

After we finished buying our dresses, we looked around at a few more stores. I hadn't had this much fun since Cassie had died. We used to do all kinds of crazy things that most would consider stupid. I remember one night we were staying at her house, and the two of us snuck out and poured bubble baths into fountains. It was a ton of fun, probably not an amazing decision, but worth it.

Who the hell wishes they stayed in more when they're on their deathbed after all? When we finally got back to our hotel room it was only nine forty-five.

"I'm exhausted," Violet announced, fighting back a yawn.

"Well then you better grab a Red Bull, because the fun is just beginning," I said, with a smirk. Claire threw her head back and gave me a confused, but worried, look.

"Harley, it's already nine forty-five," Violet whined.

"Too bad," I said.

"Harley, we can always go tomorrow," Claire said. She looked like she had something on her mind.

"But we don't know that to be a hundred percent true, look what happened to Cassie. We only have so many days on this planet, and I don't want to spend one of them wasting away in a hotel room while I'm in Vegas. Get up, get your shit together, and put your dresses on cause we're going clubbing," I said.

I was not backing down on this. I will be damned if I don't go clubbing in Vegas at least once while I'm here with my two closest friends.

"Can't argue with that," Claire said, getting up.

I looked at Violet with my best pleading face. I even brought out the puppy eyes.

"Fine, but only because I love you guys. Just one question though, how are we going to get in?" Violet asked.

I loved Violet, but she worried way too much.

"The fake IDs, duh," I said, looking at her like it was obvious.

She opened her mouth to argue, but then I gave her the look. The type of look your parents give you when they are right about something.

"Fine," Violet finally sighed.

"I knew you'd come around," I said, beaming.

It took us about half an hour to get ready. I had decided to go with a smoky eye since it matched my dress, while Violet and Claire decided to stick with lighter makeup. It was a safer choice, but cute nevertheless. We found a club called *Senor Frog's* Which sounded pretty cool. It was beach themed. The line was long, but I still dragged Violet and Claire into it. While in the horrid line Violet was freaking out a bit.

"What if they don't buy the IDs?" Violet said.

I wanted so badly to slap her, but I restrained myself. Violet and Claire are like sisters to me, as Cassie was, but that's one of the problems with sisters. You always love them at the end of the day, but sometimes you want to slap the shit out of them.

"Violet, we're young, so let's enjoy it and have some fun and stop worrying," I decided to say instead of slapping her.

I figured that being patient would get through to her a bit better. "You're right," she said, taking a shaky breath.

I could tell she just wanted to get me off of her back.

When we were finally at the front of the line a security guard asked for our IDs. I calmly handed him my "ID" followed by Claire, then Violet, and the guard let us in without question.

Once we were in the club I could feel Violet let out a huge breath. I stopped myself from going "I told you so". I thought it might be kind of bitchy. Instead I grabbed her hand and led her in the club with Claire trailing behind her.

The club was almost vibrating, it was dark with colorful lights dancing about the room, and the music was so loud I could feel it flowing through me as people were dancing and drinking everywhere I looked. It was perfect.

I could almost imagine Cassie dancing in the center of the room, almost freezing time. Cassie was never just alive, she lived. I wanted to do that.

I looked at Claire who seemed a mix of surprise and almost a confusion of what to do, then I looked to Violet, who looked captivated yet scared at the same time.

"Let's go dance!" I had to yell through the music. I had to pump them up.

They both nodded then followed me towards the center. After about thirty minutes of dancing I had worked up a thirst.

"I'll be right back. I'm going to get us drinks!" I yelled, then walked off before they could protest.

I ordered three strawberry margaritas. I had never had a margarita before, but it looked good, like an alcohol slushy, so I ordered one. I made my way back to Violet and Claire. Violet saw the drink and my hand and her eyes went wide.

"No! I can't drink that," she said, looking horrified.

I looked to Claire who looked thirsty and handed her the

drink. She looked at it then shrugged and took a sip. Violet looked shocked, then again so was I. Claire wasn't as uptight as Violet, but she wasn't exactly a "rebel".

Claire must've seen the looks on our faces.

"We're in Las Vegas doing the things that my dead sister never got to do, so just for this one trip I'm going to have fun and enjoy myself. I want to be able to say that I lived at least once in my life," she said with a shrug.

Normally I would be concerned, but we were in a club in Las Vegas, so who was I to tell her she couldn't have fun?

"Bottoms up to that," I said, taking a sip of my drink.

It really did taste like an alcohol slushy, but in a good way. Finally after a long moment Violet rolled her eyes and took a sip.

"I'm only having one though, I need to make sure that all three of us get back intact," Violet said, as if I would call her mother or report her.

"Deal," I said smiling.

I couldn't help but smile at Violet. She looked so innocent here, like a child in a high school gym class.

We began to dance again, then I got another margarita, then another. I wasn't completely sure, but if I had to guess, I would say I was pretty hammered. As I was dancing I bumped into a really cute guy. He looked a little young to be in the club, but he was cut with tan skin and brown curly hair with deep brown eyes. He looked like he definitely played a sport with his broad shoulders.

"Sorry," I said, batting my eyelashes.

He blushed a little. I was no stranger to flirting, and he was cute, so what the hell? "That's okay," he said starting to walk away.

"Wait, don't I at least get a name?" I asked. He blushed a

little and scratched his neck.

"Umm, please don't report me, but before you jump on me I'm kinda underage," he said nervously.

I laughed. He looked at me confused.

"Me too. I just turned seventeen like a month ago," I explained. "Let me guess he barely checked your ID," I said. He let out a smile. "My real name is Harley, but for the night I'm Haley," I continued. He laughed.

"I'm Estaban for the night, but my real name is Eli," he said smiling. I smiled back.

"Well, Estaban, you are quite cute," I said with a wink.

He blushed. His awkwardness just made him seem more cute in a way. "You too, Haley," he replied with a smile.

I don't know if it was the margarita, or the fact that I knew that I would most likely never see this guy again, which meant no commitment, but before I knew it my tongue was in his mouth. We went to the corner of the club for what felt like an eternity of heaven, when I felt a hand on my shoulder and looked up to see an angry Violet.

Claire

Being in Vegas still felt unreal, but a part of me still longed for my sister. Back in the hotel room I was exhausted from shopping, and a part of me didn't want to go out tonight, but then I thought back to the airport. I knew that my sister would go out and have the time of her life no matter how exhausted she was, so I sucked it up and threw my dress on.

Walking into the club I felt a sudden surge of grief. I missed her so much, so when Harley came by with drinks, I chugged it down without a second thought. I let go that night; not just because I missed Cassie, but because I couldn't stand the pain of her absence. I worked my way towards the center of the dance floor, and let the music wash over me. The floor was crowded with a bunch of young girls in party dresses, and men trying to talk to them. The sight made me laugh to myself a little bit.

I drank one drink after the other until I started to lose count. About ninety-eight percent of the time I would consider myself a pretty responsible person, but I figured I should enjoy the other two percent of the time. I thought of my sister as the liquid ran down my throat. I remembered all of the times we fought over stupid things as all sisters do. I smiled at the thoughts. As we grew older we often laughed at our past arguments. I took a long sip after that, allowing the liquid to let me forget.

I worked my way back onto the dance floor and started dancing, which I don't normally do, until I was dripping with sweat. I let my mind wander into nothing as I stumbled to another

part of the dance floor. I felt a little wobbly, but didn't let it stop me. I just kept going.
    I had a feeling that I would regret this tomorrow.

Violet

When Harley handed me a drink I already knew that I would be babysitting. After a few hours of watching them dance from afar, I decided that it was probably best to leave considering it was two in the morning.

I saw Claire dancing in a group of people. She looked drunk off her ass, so I went over and grabbed her by the wrist.

"Oh my gosh! Violet!" she said hugging me and laughing at the same time. This was going to be a long night.

"Hi, Claire, come on, it's time to go," I said, leading her away from the group of people.

"Wait, just one more song," she drawled, wobbling back to where she was.

"Claire, it's two in the morning," I said, using all of my patience.

"Woah. That's insane! We're like real party animals,." she said, starting to giggle.

She kept giggling as I dragged her to go get Harley with me. When I got to the corner Harley was with some dude making out.

Gross.

I tapped her on the shoulder, still cringing. "Come on, time to leave," I said.

"Just like five more minutes," she said turning back to mystery dude. I rolled my eyes.

"Harley, it's two in the morning," I said, my patience beginning to slip away.

"The real rock stars stay up till five," she said throwing up the rock on sign with her hands, and sticking her tongue out.

Sadly that made Claire laugh, not a cute little giggle, a laugh, and a loud one at that, which didn't stop. As my patience dissolved, I grabbed Harley and dragged her off of mystery guy, which was very difficult, then guided both Harley and Claire to the exit.

While walking away mystery guy decided to yell, "Can I get your number at least?" Harley pretended to not hear him as usual. Once we got outside Harley giggled a bit.

"That poor guy really thought I wanted a relationship." She giggled.

That made Claire start to giggle again.

"You could be a bit nicer. What's so wrong with wanting a relationship?" I said feeling a bit bad for mystery guy.

"Because then they just leave you like Rodger, or ignore you like my parents," she said with a laugh.

Even though she laughed, I could see a pain flicker through her eyes. I guess she really was drunk. I had always wondered why she never got a long term relationship before.

Rodger was her first boyfriend, she had been with him for two months when they broke up. It was also her longest relationship. He was going to leave for military camp, and wasn't going to be able to see her for a long time, so she broke up with him. If they really wanted to, they could've made it work, but it would've been hard on both of them, so she took the less painful route.

"Not everyone is like that. You just have to find the right person," I said.

"But good people also leave, look at Cassie," she said, "Good people leave all the time," she added quietly.

"Brandon never left her," I said.

She stopped and looked at me. For just a hundredth of a second I could see all of the pain in Harley. She looked at me with her deep blue eyes. They almost glowed with the neon lighting in the background.

"Well look what happened to them," she said, without breaking eye contact.

"Yeah, but if they lived through that, knowing Cassie they would get married the second they got out. Don't you ever want that, a person you can spend the rest of your life with, someone to raise children with?" I asked.

Part of me longed for that myself.

"Of course I do, but they always leave," she said, looking at the ground. "They always leave," she mumbled, looking down.

The rest of the walk was silent.

When we got to the hotel Harley and Claire passed out in their dresses and makeup. I went over and took their shoes off. I changed into my pajamas and washed my face before going to bed.

Throughout the night I could hear one or the other, sometimes both of them, get up and go throw up.

I woke up at about eight in the morning. Claire and Harley were out cold. I smiled to myself. If only they saw themselves last night. I decided that I should make recovering for them a little bit easier. I got up and got ready, then I went downstairs and walked towards the hotel next to us.

There was a tram there that went to *Treasure Island* which was a hotel with a little convenience store in it. I made my way through the bottom floor of the hotel, aka the casino, which reeked of cigarettes and alcohol. I never understood how people drink at eight in the morning, but then again it was Vegas.

I made my way to the convenience store in the back and got some Pedialyte, three bottled coffees, a loaf of bread, butter, and jam. I made my way back through the cigarette-smelling casino and walked back to the tram. I got back to the hotel at about nine fifteen. Harley and Claire were still asleep. They were not morning people, even without the hangover.

This is going to be "fun", I thought to myself, dropping the bag on a nightstand. I went over to wake up Harley and Claire.

"I have food," I said, nudging Harley.

"Just five more minutes," she whined, rolling over.

"Come on, Harls, get up," I pleaded.

"Fine," she said, rolling back over.

I let out a sigh of relief and went over and opened the curtains. Harley squinted and put her hands over her face.

"Why is it so bright?" she complained.

"Ugg, what time is it?" Claire grumbled, rubbing her eyes. The light must have woken her up.

"Nine fifteen, now get up, come on, let's go," I said, walking back over to the bag from the convenience store.

"Omg, I feel like I'm dying," Claire groaned. I decided to ignore that.

As they got up I put butter and jam on three slices of bread, poured two glasses of Pedialyte, and set up the three bottles of coffee.

"I am never drinking again," Claire groaned, sitting down. I laughed a little, sitting down next to her.

"So maybe Violet isn't so dumb after all," I said, smirking.

Claire smiled and rolled her eyes. While the three of us ate, we laughed and talked about the amazing party.

"So what's the plan for today?" I asked, excited to see what else Vegas can offer. Harley smiled and looked at us.

"Have you ever heard of Omega Mart?" she asked

"What's that?" I asked, a bit confused, and wondering if there was still some margarita in her system.

"Oh my gosh! Cassie would be ecstatic right now," Claire squealed before Harley got a chance to answer me.

"I know." Harley beamed with pride.

She looked over at me and must have seen the confused look on my face, so she started to explain what "Omega Mart" was.

"It's like an alien-themed grocery store, but there are secret passages that lead underground throughout the store, and it's not an actual grocery store. Once you get to the under part of the store there's a bunch of puzzles you solve that go along with a storyline, and there's a bunch of art, they even have a slide. Most people just go for the cool rooms though," Harley explained, smiling ear to ear.

She looked so proud of herself.

"Okay, that does sound pretty cool," I admitted. "Just please tell me it doesn't involve drinking; I really don't feel like babysitting again," I pleaded.

I just wanted to have a fun day without being insane.

"Don't worry I'm never drinking again," Claire assured me, taking a sip of her coffee.

Harley and I laughed. I wondered if she remembered last night, dancing with a bunch of drunk sweaty people.

"I think I'm going to take a bit of a break," Harley said. I smiled and rolled my eyes. "Don't worry, I'm pretty sure they don't serve drinks," Harley assured me.

"Well then let's go," I said, smiling.

Claire

Last night was one of the best nights I ever had, my body was slightly regretting it, but I wasn't. Part of me kept telling myself that I wasn't going to drink, but when we were in line I couldn't help but remember the promise I made Violet in the airport. I thought about how badly Cassie wanted to go to the places we were going to on this trip. The whole point of this trip was to live for her, and I knew damn well that my sister would never go to Vegas and not have the time of her life, so I figured that since she can't, I will.

I knew that when Violet said that she was only going to have one drink, she meant it. That's just how Violet is, I knew she would be responsible, so I drank without worry or care. I danced to the feeling that for one night, one precious night, I would have the time of my life without worrying, or being uptight. I let go. Sadly there was a consequence; I was now hung over and felt like shit, but in my opinion it was one hundred percent worth it.

When Violet woke me up by so kindly opening the blinds my entire body cringed. As soon as I sat up my head began to throb. I don't know what death feels like, but I can imagine that that feeling wasn't far from it.

When I heard we were going to Omega Mart I decided to chug the Pedi Light, that was kindly provided by Violet, and suck it up.

How the hell did people do this every weekend?

Once we got to Omega Mart it was about ten o'clock. I

looked out of the Uber window as we pulled up with awe. Omega Mart was unreal, all of the decorations were unique, and looked totally realistic. It was all alien themed, with stuff like tattooed chicken, and vegetable wallets. Once we got inside, we paid our way in and got to exploring. We found a secret entrance right away, which was in a "freezer".

We ended up spending two hours there trying to solve the "mystery", in which we eventually gave up, and just admired all of the decorations and art.

It was twelve o'clock when we finally got outside. I heard my stomach start to growl walking through the door. We walked outside and waited for an Uber.

"That was awesome!" I said, as Harley took a seat on the curb.

I can see why Cassie wanted to go here so bad, she would have totally loved it.

"I know, and we totally did 'awesome' at solving the 'mystery'," Harley said with a laugh. I couldn't help but laugh myself.

"Yeah I had a lot of fun," Violet chimed in.

She smoothed her skirt down and took a seat next to me. "Is anyone else starving, or is it just me?" I asked.

All three of us laughed.

"I could definitely go for some food," Violet agreed.

"Well that's good, because that happens to be our next stop," Harley said, with a mischievous grin.

"And where would this happen to be?" I asked curiously. Harley had a huge grin painted on her face.

"The Sugar Factory," she said with a smile. I couldn't help but smile.

Even though I've never been big on traveling, Cassie once told me about this place where they had milkshakes as big as your head, and since then me and Cassie had always wanted to go there.

What can I say? I have a sweet tooth.

"Thank you, Harls." I smiled.

She smiled back. I knew it was on the bucket list, but I suspected that Cassie wasn't the only reason she put it on the trip.

"What's Sugar Factory?" Violet asked.

"It's this restaurant where they have a bunch of crazy sweets, and real food, like hamburgers with colored buns," I explained.

I probably sounded like a little kid.

"That does sound pretty cool," Violet said.

I smiled. I turned my head to the side to see our Uber arriving just in time.

All three of us hopped in and told the driver where to. I was ecstatic the whole way there, practically bouncing in my seat. I know it is a stupid thing to get excited over, but I was never really big on traveling, and always thought Cassie to be crazy for loving it so much, but now that I was out of Ohio, and doing something I wanted to do with my best friends, I could finally start to understand why she wanted to see the world so much, because there is a lot to see.

When we pulled up to the restaurant it looked just like the pictures that Cassie had showed me. I smiled at the memory of us in middle school dreaming of giant milkshakes. Thankfully, Harley had made reservations, so we got right in. I could smell sugar as soon as we walked in, like a kitchen just after baking cookies.

I took a deep breath and looked around to see a bunch of smiling faces with people laughing, or just enjoying the food, and in a way it made me think of my sister, but not in a sad way. Obviously I missed her, but I smiled, remembering all of the times where she brought joy to people around her, and I could picture her sitting next to Harley laughing along with the rest of us, and probably ordering a giant milkshake, bringing joy to the others around us. When I pictured this, it wasn't like the other times, it was like she was almost here, with us.

"Claire?" I looked up to see Harley's hand waving in front of my face.

"Sorry," I said, snapping back into reality.

"You're good, is everything okay? You look like you just aced a test or something," Harley said, looking at me slightly concerned.

I smiled.

"I'm okay," I assured them.

"In that case what are we going to get to drink?" Harley asked with a big smile.

We had a tradition that whenever we go out to a real restaurant, not fast food, we always got the same drink. I looked down at the menu scanning our drink options. I saw a few alcoholic ones, and decided to stay clear of those. My body did not need another hangover.

"How about the watermelon patch one?" I asked.

"It looks amazing," Violet said, licking her lips.

"Sounds good to me," Harley agreed.

When the waitress came by we ordered our drinks along with a basket of fries. When the waitress came back with our drinks and fries we all ordered. I got chicken and waffles, Harley got rainbow sliders, and Violet got a club sandwich. The drinks were amazing, but sadly mine did not last very long.

When our waitress came back with our food I was practically

drooling. The food was also amazing. I loved breakfast food.

After we finished I was stuffed, but couldn't resist dessert. We decided to share the Giggles Snickers Milkshake, which was once again amazing. Even between the three of us we couldn't finish it.

I felt very full walking out of the restaurant. We decided to walk to our hotel after our feast. We rested for a while, while Harley made reservations at our next pitstop. I took a nap, which felt like a food coma. When I woke up it was already five o'clock.

"Good morning," Harley said with a laugh.

"So what are we doing next?" I asked.

I sat up and took a big stretch.

"We're going to dinner at seven forty-five, but first I have a surprise," Harley said happily.

"Well what would the surprise be?" I asked, my eyebrows raised.

Harley just shrugged.

"You'll need jeans and a shirt for this one," was all she said.

She had officially piqued my interest. She got up and walked to the other side of the room, leaving me to wonder.

When I finally couldn't take it any more I begged Harley to tell me. "What is it? I give up," I pleaded.

She just smiled and shrugged again. I angrily rolled my eyes. "Harley," I whined.

I kept whining until she finally cracked. "Calm down, I'll tell you," she finally agreed. I smiled smugly, feeling accomplished.

"Glad you could come to that decision," I said.

"I could always change my mind," Harley shot back. She was now the one smiling.

"Fine," I mumbled, once again rolling my eyes. Her

mischievous smile grew.

Ug.

"We are going to a dolphin show at the Mirage," Harley finally let out. "Are you happy now?" she asked sarcastically.

"Yes I am," I said, grinning. She rolled her eyes.

"We're going where?" Violet gasped, sticking her head out of the bathroom, where she was previously doing her makeup.

She loved dolphins for some weird reason.

"Hold on, I'm almost done," she said, rushing back into the bathroom. Me and Harley laughed.

When we left the hotel, we decided to walk since we were right next door. The Mirage, of course, had a casino on the bottom floor. Once we got past the casino we found our way to a giant hall full of stores. The hall led to the pool/dolphin area.

The pool area was gorgeous. It made you feel like you were at a tropical island. There was a giant pool with plenty of lounge chairs, and beautiful palm trees. A part of me wanted to ditch the shows and go swimming.

I looked over at Violet, who was practically bouncing up and down like a little kid. As we got to the dolphin area, I saw a gift shop. I now knew where I would be spending money later.

The dolphin show was awesome. It was at a giant pool with about three dolphins doing tricks. After it was over we walked over to the big cat area. It wasn't a show like the dolphins, but it was still pretty cool. In one cage there was a big black cat asleep, with another one trying to wake it up. The one asleep was not having it.

"Hey Harley it's you," I said, pointing at the cat.

Violet let out a giggle. Harley smiled and rolled her eyes. "Like you're one to talk," she responded.

We all laughed at that one.

We decided that we had had enough wildlife for one day, and started walking back the way we came.

"Wait!" I exclaimed as we passed the gift shop. "Can we go in?" I pleaded.

Harley laughed.

"You are unnecessarily dramatic, and go ahead," Harley said.

We made our way through the gift shop. There was a pile of miniature stuffed animals. I laughed as I picked up one that looked like the sleepy cat.

"Harley," I said laughing, holding up the stuffed animal.

We both started laughing, and decided to each get one. Violet ended up getting a dolphin one. We paid and left.

"That was so much fun," Violet said.

We were now back on the strip, walking back to our hotel.

"Well I'm glad you guys liked it," Harley said. "Hopefully lunch didn't fill you guys up too much, by the way, because we're going to the Paris for dinner," Harley continued.

"I don't think we're going to be able to fit in those bikinis after this," I said with a laugh. Harley and Violet laughed along with me.

"Oh no, looks like we'll have to get one-pieces," Violet said with a tone of sarcasm. Harley rolled her eyes.

"Or we can just suck it in and squeeze in," Harley suggested.

We all giggled. Once we got back to the hotel we all got ready for dinner. It was a bit difficult to do makeup when sharing a mirror with two other people, but we managed. Once we were finally ready we decided to walk to The Paris.

It was beautiful, there was a fake Eiffel Tower which was home to the restaurant. The view from the window next to our table was stunning. We had a view of the whole city, which glowed with lights, making it appear illuminating. I felt a little awestruck as we sat down. The menu looked equally as amazing, but sadly I was still a bit full from lunch.

"Okay so this might sound dumb, but do you guys want to share a beef wellington?" I asked. Harley laughed.

"You still full from lunch?" Harley asked.

"Just a little," I admitted.

"I am too," Violet said sheepishly.

"I think we all are," Harley said.

We all laughed. I could tell that it was going to be a fun night.

Harley

I was stuffed after lunch, so when Claire suggested that we share at dinner I was actually relieved, but she didn't need to know that. I remember her telling me that she and Cassie wanted to go to Sugar Factory someday when we were kids, so when we decided we were going to Vegas on this trip I knew that I had to book it. In a way this trip was starting to really bring Claire and Violet out of their shells, well not much for Violet, but it's progress.

Dinner was amazing even though we didn't eat that much. I sat back with a full stomach and looked out the window, and enjoyed the view.

"That was delicious, I cannot wait to sleep when we get back to the hotel," Violet said.

This was our last night in Vegas, and I was not ending it on a dinner. I had one more surprise. "Actually I have one more trick up my sleeve," I said, with a grin. Claire smiled and rolled her eyes.

"Harley, you always have tricks up your sleeve," Claire said smiling. I shrugged.

"Maybe I do," I said.

"Just please tell me you two won't get drunk," Violet groaned.

"We will not be, thank you very much," I said.

"We are going on a ride," I said.

They looked confused for a minute, then Violet's eyes lit up with realization and terror. "Harley, please don't," she whined.

Claire still looked confused.

"We are going on the roller coaster at New York New York," I announced.

"Oh, yeah that sounds fun, a bit scary, but I'm down," Claire said.

Violet on the other hand looked terrified, she has never been a big fan of roller coasters. "Harley, have you seen how high up that thing is?" Violet said, while most likely thinking up an excuse.

I could tell she was panicking.

"Vi, we're doing this trip for Cassie, and riding that ride is specifically on her bucket list," I said. It came out a little more harsh than I intended.

"Well guess what, I'm not Cassie, and I'm not brave as her, and I never was, but guess what. I don't care because that's what makes Cassie Cassie, and me me," Violet spat out.

She looked slightly angry now.

"No one is asking you to be Cassie. We are simply asking you to go on a roller coaster for her since she can't," I said.

I was a bit angry, but tried not to show it. She was just scared after all. She looked at me. I could almost hear her brain ticking.

"For her?" I spoke softly.

I looked right into her emerald green eyes, using my own to say a silent plea. "Fine," she finally said without breaking eye contact.

"Thank you," I said, pairing it with a soft smile. She looked at me uneasy.

"It's just a ride," Claire said, placing a reassuring hand lightly on her shoulder.

"Okay," Violet said softly.

I wish Cassie could see her right now.

When we got to New York New York it was packed. To get to the roller coaster you had to walk through the casino floor and go up to the second level. The bottom level was totally awesome, it looked like an inside version of New York, there was even a taxi on the roof. It smelled like the rest of Vegas, reeking with cigarette smoke. As we walked up to the roller coaster floor we looked at the hotel in awe, well me and Claire did at least. Violet looked pale. I could tell she was panicking.

Once we got up to the desk I could practically see the sweat dripping down Violet's forehead. She was practically shaking as we bought our tickets. Maybe I shouldn't have forced her.

"Vi, it's a ride that lasts like ten seconds," Claire said, trying to calm her down. Violet was quick with her response.

"Actually it's three minutes," she responded quickly. I could tell she did her research.

"Well since you looked it up, you know that it's completely safe," I said, trying to comfort her. A part of me was starting to feel like an asshole, but I wanted Violet to not have any regrets.

"Yes, but still scary as hell. What if we're that one in a million that goes flying off, or gets stuck upside down or—" I cut her off before she could finish.

"But what if we're not? You like math, the odds are highly on our side. One day we won't get to do this. Cassie lived her whole life wanting to do this, but she was never able to. Violet, when you're all grown up and have some boring job, with a boring life, where you have to be an adult level of responsibility, don't you want to be able to say that you lived, just for this trip, just for twelve days? We're young, we're supposed to be stupid and do crazy things," I said.

She looked at me. I looked into her eyes.

"Of course I do, but I don't normally live like this. It's hard to just let go when you've been holding on for so long," she said.

There was a sense of remorse in her tone, almost as if she lost something she never had. "You get twelve days to be a stupid teenager, with no responsibilities or AP classes, and your mom is a bit far away, so please just let go for twelve days, then you can go back to living a safe and content life in Ohio," I said.

She took a deep breath, and looked away for a moment. "Deal," she finally said, not looking back.

After about twenty minutes of waiting in line, and Violet trying to compose herself, we finally made it to the front of the line. They sat two to a row, so I volunteered to sit with a stranger. It was the least I could do.

Violet closed her eyes as the cars approached. Claire turned to face me and Violet. "Can I admit something?" she asked.

She told us before either of us could answer.

"I am also a bit terrified," she confessed, with a nervous laugh.

"Chicken," I teased.

We all let out a nervous laugh.

I've never had a problem with roller coasters, in fact I loved them, but Violet always hated them. I've understood why they may seem intimidating to some, but personally I've always loved the adrenaline rush. I guess Cassie felt the same since this was on the list.

We strapped in and the roller coaster started. I could feel my pulse quicken as adrenaline pumped through my veins, it was one of my favorite feelings. As we climbed to the top of the first, and biggest, drop, we had a view of the whole strip. At the top the city was a blur of bright lights, and loud streets filled with people. I almost forgot where I was for a moment. When I stopped admiring the view, I realized that we were at the top. I put my hands up as the coaster descended, as I heard Violet scream.

As I stepped off of the ride I felt amazing with all of the adrenaline still coursing through my system. I felt a gust of air blow past me as Claire sprinted towards the nearest trash can.

Maybe we should've done this before we ate. Violet slowly got off shaking, looking like she had seen a ghost. After Claire was done... revisiting her dinner, she walked back over to us.

"Even though I puked my guts out, it was still a ton of fun," Claire said, starting to laugh. I started to laugh too. Violet did not.

"Hey, Vi, you okay?" I asked. She looked up.

"That was the most terrifying experience of my life, but I'm glad I did it. I may have almost peed myself, but at least I can say I conquered my fear," she said, smiling weakly.

I smiled.

"Cassie would have been proud," I said.

She smiled as a tear escaped from her eyes.

I only wish that Cassie were here. She would have had so much fun on the coaster, and she really would have been proud of Violet.

The walk back to our hotel was quiet. It wasn't the awkward, or heavy, kind of silence. It was the nice peaceful kind, the kind that was almost comforting. Since we got here something had changed. It felt like we were really starting to live. Cassie would be so happy for us if she could be here.

When we got back to the hotel I was exhausted. Claire and Violet looked like they felt the same way. After I got ready for bed and washed my face, I face-planted into the bed. That night was the first night since Cassie died that I fell asleep happy.

In the morning I woke up and smiled. When I first heard that Cassie died I thought that I'd never be happy again, but for the first time since Cassie died I was truly happy, then I started to think about her. The hurt started to take over again. I closed my eyes. I pictured her. I pictured our middle school soccer tryouts. We were both totally awkward.

"Are you ready?" I could hear her voice so clearly.

"Duh." I could still hear her laugh.

It was loud. I smiled. She had always had a loud laugh. The memory faded. I suddenly became aware of reality. All the feelings that I felt on the night that she died came rushing back. It was like she had died all over again.

I stopped myself and shook it off. If I kept telling myself that she's basically here, then she would be. I just had to keep remembering. My stomach started to growl.

"Sound's like someone is hungry," Violet said walking out of the bathroom with a laugh.

I jumped a bit. If she knew that I still felt like shit over Cassie she would force me to talk about my feelings and force sappy stuff and emotions on me, which would make me a complete wreck, which would ruin the vacation, so I painted on a smile.

"Starving actually," I said.

Claire rolled over with a groan. "What time is it?" she complained.

"Time for you to get up," I said putting my cold foot on her back.

She jumped up with a yelp, then threw her pillow at me as I fell back laughing. "Just for that I get the bathroom first," she said sprinting to the bathroom.

She knew that if she walked I would end up racing her for it, but since she got such a head start I didn't have a chance.

"I get it first tonight then," I yelled back, as the bathroom door closed.

I checked the time on my phone, which read six forty-five in the morning. I guess I was still used to Ohio time. After what seemed like an eternity Claire finally stepped out of the bathroom. "All yours," she said.

"I am definitely getting it first tonight," I said as I closed the door.

I brushed my teeth, washed my face, and put on a navy tank top and black jean shorts with my black high top converse.

"Where are we going for breakfast?" I asked, stepping out of the bathroom.

"I could go for some pancakes," Claire responded.

"Is Denny's okay?" Violet suggested.

"I'm good with that," Claire said.

"Sounds good," I agreed.

By the time we got to Denny's it was seven thirty. We all got coffee. Me and Violet got French toast, while Claire got pancakes.

"I can't believe that it's our last day," Violet said between bites of French toast.

"Me too," Claire said while scarfing down her pancakes.

"I can't believe you went on the roller coaster last night," I said, smiling. Violet rolled her eyes, trying to hide her smile.

"I'm surprised you 'weren't scared'," Claire said putting air quotes up. I smiled.

"I wasn't," I confidently assured her. "Least I kept my dinner down," I said, smirking. She kicked me under the table.

"Ouch," I yelped.

"Bitch," I said with a smile. She smiled back.

"I don't know how you guys didn't throw up after all we ate,"

Claire said.

We finished our breakfast, and decided to go shopping one last time before we left. We didn't end up buying anything, but we did have a lot of fun. We marveled at the large amounts of stores, and the amazing structure of the building. I thought of the trip so far as we walked outside.

I laughed to myself walking back to the hotel. Who would've thought that Violet and Claire would actually let loose a bit. I wish Cassie could've seen it. I shook the thought from my head, I had to stay positive and do what she would want me to do. I looked at the massive buildings around us that had mesmerized us when we first saw them. I know that Las Vegas is referred to as "Sin City", but people often don't realize how beautiful the city actually is, and the wonders it does for people, plus the pirates are totally awesome.

I think that Vegas is misjudged. Everyone has to party or let loose at some point in their life, and this city brings it out of people.

I was glad that we were able to come here, a part of me actually wanted to go to college here. I could already picture it, me at UNLV, driving to the strip on weekends, partying, and shopping. It was perfect.

By the time we made it to the hotel it was already nine o'clock. That gave about an hour to pack and head out. I finished packing in about fifteen minutes.

"Stay here, I'm going to go get our rental car," I said fishing in my bag for my hotel key.

"Sounds good," Claire said, sorting through her suitcase.

"Are you sure you want to go by yourself?" Violet asked worriedly. She sounded like a mother.

"I'll be fine," I assured her, as I walked out the door.

When I got to the lobby I ordered an Uber. Once inside I told the driver the name of the rental car company.

"Did you come out here all by yourself?" the driver asked, with concern in her voice. She looked to be in her early twenties, maybe even still in college.

"No, I'm just picking up the rental car," I said.

"You should be more careful; I could've been a total weirdo," she said, letting out a breath. I laughed.

"Well are you?" I asked.

"No," she admitted.

"Well then I guess it worked out." I laughed.

She cracked a smile. She had shoulder length curly blond hair, and bright blue eyes. "So have you lived here long?" I asked to start small talk.

"It's my fifth year here. I just finished college last year at UNLV, and now me and my boyfriend are saving some money to move to Cali," she explained.

"That's cool, I was just thinking about going to UNLV after high school."

"It's amazing there, if you do decide on it, you'll love it."

"So what part of California are you moving to?" I asked, changing the subject.

"Clovis, my boyfriend, wants to teach at his old high school there. It's a small town near Fresno."

"That's awesome."

"So what brings you to Vegas?" she asked.

I laughed when she asked me that. If only she knew. "Just an old friend," I said, looking out the window. We pulled up to the rent-a-car place.

"Have fun with your friend," she said as I got out of the car.

"Thank you, and good luck with Clovis."

"Thanks," she said driving off.

I smiled walking into the rent-a-car place, thinking how Cassie would have answered her question if the roles were reversed. She probably would have made up some crazy story.

I got in line and checked in.

"Here you go," the lady said, handing me a key.

"Is it the car I put in a request for?" I asked with a devious grin.

"Go see for yourself," she said.

I smiled and walked off after thanking her. To my surprise, it was the exact car I had requested. I couldn't help but smile.

Claire and Violet were in for a fun ride.

Violet

I answered my phone to the sound of Harley's voice. I had just finished packing and tidying up the hotel room.

"Hey, we're all packed up and ready to go," I said, as Claire and I exited the room.

"Perfect, I'm outside. Can you bring my luggage down?"

"Yeah."

"Thanks, Vi."

"No problem," I said hanging up the phone.

Maybe it was just me, but Harley seemed a bit more excited than usual, which meant we were either going to do something stupid, something fun, or a little bit of both. I guess I'd just have to wait to find out.

When me and Claire made it downstairs I could immediately see what Harley was excited about.

"How'd you talk the rent-a-car company into lending you this?" Claire asked.

"By telling them how amazing of a driver I was," Harley said, flipping her hair over her shoulder sarcastically.

Claire rolled her eyes, while smiling. Harley opened the trunk and we started to load stuff in. It was a bit of a squeeze, but it was actually more roomy than it appeared. I volunteered to sit in the back so I could have more room, Harley obviously wanted to drive, and Claire took the passenger seat.

"So what exact model is this car?" I asked. Harley smiled.

"2019 Maserati, which is obviously a convertible," she said.

"I like the color," I said. The Maserati was a gleaming white, I thought it suited the car.

"Me too," Harley said, with a wild grin on her face.

"I didn't know they even rented these," Claire said, looking around the interior of the car.

"They do for a price," Harley said, starting the car.

"Harls! How much did it cost?" I asked, shocked.

"Calm down, my parents did a lot of surgeries this year," she said.

I often forgot that Harley came from money. Though her parents were both high-level surgeons that made plenty of money, most of their riches came from blood money. Her grandparents were very rich farmers. I'm sure they had offered to pay for most of this vacation. Claire and I also came from money, but more like upper middle class, nothing compared to Harley. My mom and I made more than enough to get by, but we weren't exactly rich, and Claire made a bit more than us.

"You didn't even hear the best part about the car," Harley said, with a huge grin.

"Oh boy," Claire said. I laughed.

"It has Bluetooth," Harley said.

I knew that she already hooked her phone up to it. I watched as Harley turned the volume up and put the top down. As we drove off I looked behind us to see Las Vegas one more time. Even though it was about ten in the morning, it was still as beautiful as ever.

We spent the next hour laughing, singing along to music at the top of our lungs, and admiring the scenery as we drove to LA.

"I can't wait till we get there," I said, practically bouncing in my seat.

We still had hours till LA, but I couldn't help but feel excited.

Harley laughed a bit.

"Well that's a shame, because you're going to have to wait a few hours," she said from the driver's seat.

Claire smiled, and started clicking on the screen on the car.

"Well, looks like I'm in charge of making sure we don't die of boredom," she said as she hooked up her phone to the Bluetooth.

"Woah! Who do you think you are changing my music?" Harley exclaimed. Claire laughed.

"Sorry, Harls, but you have to focus on the road," she said.

Harley groaned as some country song filled the silence. Harley hated country, so did Cassie, and I wasn't so fond of it myself, but Claire loved it.

"Booo!" Harley said.

"I agree with the boo," I said from the back seat. Claire rolled her eyes.

"Fine. You guys are haters," she said as she changed the playlist.

"Much better," Harley said, turning the volume up as "Come and Get your Love" played.

Harley listened to all kinds of music. Even though she didn't listen to oldies very often, she did enjoy them when they came on. We all sang along at the top of our lungs, even Claire. I couldn't help but smile looking around. I was with my two best friends on a road trip to LA.

Then I felt an emptiness next to me. Claire usually sat in the back with me, but Cassie wasn't here so she was up front. It was only a second that I realized that she wasn't here. It was funny how that worked, as soon as I feel relieved of the pain, it comes rushing back. I looked to my right. I closed my eyes and stuck my head a bit more out of the car, letting myself feel the wind, my brain drowned out by the music, I let myself feel my emotions. I let myself feel every bit of hurt, every bit of wanting to see my friend, every part of me that missed her, I let myself go, and let it go with the wind.

I opened my eyes, I knew that I would still feel the pain at one point or another, but I also knew that if I just kept fighting my feelings, and trying to push them down, I would never truly get over this. I closed my eyes again and let my brain go with the wind.

About two hours later we came to a stop. We were at a restaurant called In-N-OUT. I had heard of it before, but being from Ohio I had never tried it. We got out and walked inside. It had white walls with red piping, the tables were white, with red booths and stools. We all ordered cheeseburgers, fries, and milkshakes. Harley let out a small laugh.

"What is it?" I asked.

"Cassie put this place on the bucket list." She smiled.

"Isn't this a chain?" I asked.

"Yeah, she could've gotten it anywhere on the west coast, but still put it on the list." She laughed. That made me smile. Cassie always found aww in little things. Claire sat down holding three milkshakes. Harley and Claire got chocolate, but I got strawberry. A few minutes later Claire went to get our food. The burgers were amazing.

"Okay, I can see why she put it on the list," I said, taking a bite of my hamburger.

"Me too," Harley agreed, between bites of food.

"Wait, she put this place on the list?" Claire asked.

"Yeah," Harley and I answered at the same time.

"But isn't it a—"

"Yeah," I said cutting her off. She started laughing.

"Sounds like my sister," she said with a smile. We all smiled.

After we finished eating we hopped back in the car, and started back on the road again. The rest of the drive was, like the beginning of it, singing along, laughing, and enjoying the scenery of the drive. We arrived in LA at about two forty-five. There were definitely a lot of people. There was also a lot of traffic, but thankfully we still made it.

It felt like we spent more time in LA traffic than getting there. Thankfully we finally pulled up to our hotel after what seemed like days in the car.

We were staying in Anaheim, near Disneyland. When I got out of the car my legs almost gave out from under me. I weakly wobbled to help Harley with the luggage. Once we were checked in we made our way to our room and started to unpack.

"What do you guys think so far?" Claire asked.

"And I thought Vegas was crowded," Harley retorted. I smacked her in the arm.

"It's LA. What did you expect?" I said.

"Fair enough," she said.

"Ignore grumpy over there, I think it's pretty cool," Claire said. "All right, I'm done over here, so where to?"

That put a smile on Harley's face. "I'm so glad you asked," she said.

We made our way down stairs, and got in the car.

"Where are we going?" I asked, climbing into the backseat. Harley smiled.

"Hollywood Walk," she said, with a grin painted across her face. Claire and I looked at each other with smiles on our faces.

"This is why I love LA," I said. Harley rolled her eyes, but smiled.

"I guess it's not that bad," she admitted.

"So who was right?" Claire asked, grinning ear to ear.

"Let's at least check it out first," Harley said.

The drive over there was a bit long because of the traffic, but I didn't mind this time.

When we got to the walk it was unbelievable. The sidewalk was black, with all of the stars for celebrities.

"Okay we have to get a picture," I said, pulling out my phone.

I went over and asked some lady to take our picture. We all huddled up and smiled. After the lady gave me my phone back we all looked through the photos, looking for the one where we looked the best. After arguing for twenty minutes of which photo looked the best we finally settled on the one that was taken second to last.

"You're lucky I look good in that one," Harley said. Claire rolled her eyes.

"Well either way it's going on Instagram," Claire said, as she posted the picture. Harley rolled her eyes.

"Okay so where to?" I asked.

"Oh my gosh, I think I know what we're doing," Claire said, with a huge smile. I looked at them dumbly.

"Well what is it?" I asked, confused.

"Star Tours," Harley said, filling me in.

"Oh, duh. That would make sense," I said, smacking my palm into my forehead.

Claire giggled.

"I thought you were an honors student," Claire teased. I blushed, slightly embarrassed.

"Come on, we're going to miss our tour," Harley said.

Star Tours was a tour bus that covered a bunch of

information, and places having to do with celebrities. It was super touristy, but it was on the list.

The tour was a ton of fun, a bit cheesy, but fun.

"Dang, you can't do anything as a celebrity without someone knowing," I said, feeling a bit bad for celebrities.

"Yeah, that must suck," Claire agreed.

"Yeah, they are only beloved by millions, and are extremely wealthy to help make up for it," Harley said.

Claire rolled her eyes.

"You know I'm not wrong," Harley said. Claire rolled her eyes again.

"You can still have sympathy," she shot back.

"So what are we doing next?" I asked, changing the subject.

"Okay so this one is actually not on the list, in fact it would most likely never be," Harley said, turning to me.

I raised an eyebrow. There wasn't much that Cassie wouldn't try, so the fact that it would never be on the list made me a bit nervous.

"There's a sushi place on Sunset Blvd. It has a conveyor belt that you just pick the food off of, then at the end you put your plates in a little machine," she explained.

"Oh, you scared me," I said, feeling myself relax again.

Cassie was allergic to sushi, and most seafood for that matter, so she never went to seafood, or sushi, places for obvious reasons. The rest of us loved sushi, but tried to avoid it when we were with her.

We decided to drive to the restaurant for safety reasons. Sunset Blvd was not exactly Ohio. Thankfully it only took us about ten minutes.

When we got to Sunset Blvd, it was crowded with a bunch of college kids. UCLA was right by here, so I wasn't exactly surprised. The street was lined with cool stores and restaurants. There was what appeared to be a food truck, with a massively long line. We walked until we came up to a sushi restaurant. We walked inside to find a giant conveyor belt with plates of sushi, moving the plates to pass by each table. We sat down at a booth.

"What can I get you ladies to drink?" a what appeared to be a twentyish man asked. We all looked at each other, thinking the same thing.

"Shirley Temple," we all said unanimously.

"All right then. So the way this place works is you just grab whatever you want off the conveyor, then when you finish you place it in the slot at the end of your table and pay on the screen. The plates say what roll is on it, and the prices are organized based on the color of the plate. I'll be right back with your drinks, and to answer any questions," he said, starting to walk off.

"Thank you," I called.

"He was pretty cute," Harley said, staring at him as he walked off.

"That's what you were thinking as he was telling us how to get food?" Claire asked.

"I was partly listening. Grab food, eat food, put plates in machine," Harley said. "It's not rocket science. I should be able to enjoy the view." Harley grabbed a plate off of the conveyor belt and placed it on the table.

"See, no mathematical problems involved," she said.

Claire rolled her eyes. I tried to hide my laughter, but failed.

"Besides, he looks like the best snack here," Harley said, watching him at another table. Claire gagged.

"Oh they have a noodle plate!" I said.

I loved noodles. Harley grabbed the plate and set it in front of me. "Thank you!" I said, opening the lid.

I could already tell we weren't going to be able to fit into our jeans tomorrow.

After sharing about seven plates of sushi between the three of us we were finally full, plus I ate my noodle plate.

"You think Cas would be mad if we went here with her?" I asked.

"Nah, she would probably try to suck it up for us. She would just have noodles," Harley said. While Cassie only had allergic reactions if she actually ate seafood, and sushi, if it smelled strongly it would only make her nauseous.

"Sounds about right," Claire said, smiling at the memory.

"Remember how we found out she was also allergic to sushi," I said, starting to laugh.

"The poor kid was clueless," Harley said between laughs.

We all started laughing until we couldn't breath.

In the fifth grade a little boy had a crush on Cassie, and one day he had sushi for lunch, and all of the kids kept asking him for some. He said no to everyone, and he looked at Cassie, who didn't ask him, and he offered her a piece. She had an allergic reaction, but thankfully had an EpiPen on her. The boy felt horrible, especially since he was in love with her. When Cassie was still here we used to joke about it all the time.

After we placed all of our plates in the machine we paid, and left. When we walked outside, the street was even more busy than when we first got here. I felt a cool breeze. I could get used to this weather.

We passed by a club, Harley looked at it and smirked.

"No. I am not doing that again," I said grabbing Harley by the wrist, and dragging her away from the club.

I could hear her laughing behind me. Thankfully she must have decided to take pity on me and let me drag her away from the club, instead of fighting.

We got back to the hotel around ten forty-five. After all three of us went through our nightly routines we all passed out relatively quickly. The last thing I thought of falling asleep was a memory of the three of us and Cassie at Taco Bell talking and laughing about how she found out she was allergic to sushi. I smiled to myself, and drifted into sleep.

Claire

I woke up to the sound of someone walking around the hotel room. I jolted awake, and looked up to see Harley trying to sneak out of the room.

"And just where do you think you're going!" I whisper-yelled.

She was dressed in a tank top and leggings. She practically jumped out of her skin. "You scared the shit out of me!" she whisper-yelled back.

I looked at the clock, which read 1.27.

"Do you have any idea what time it is?" I whispered.

"I know. I couldn't sleep. I'm just going to go work out for a bit."

"Harley it's 1.27 in the morning, even though we're in a nice area you are like a hundred and twenty pounds. No offense, but if someone gives you trouble, you will most likely not be able to defend yourself."

"But I'm fast, so I'll just kick them and run. I don't have to kick their ass to stay safe," she replied.

I rolled my eyes. What the hell was she thinking? "That's not how that works."

"Well I'll let you know how it goes," she said, starting to open the door.

"Harley, wait." She stopped. "I already lost one sister, I can't lose another one." When I said it I could feel water building up in my eyes; I blinked them away.

She looked at me, something in her face softened. "I promise I'll be okay," she assured me.

I looked into her deep blue eyes, using my own eyes to plead. I couldn't lose someone else. "You can't promise that, look at what happened to Cassie," I whispered.

It was so quiet, even I barely heard it. She looked away then back to me. Guilt washed over her face.

"Okay." She closed the door and walked back to her suitcase.

She disappeared into the bathroom, holding the pajamas she was wearing before. A moment later she came out in them. We usually changed in front of each other without batting an eye, since we grew up together, so I knew that she had something on her mind. I had never seen Harley cry, nor had Violet. She had only cried in front of Cassie, so when she came out of the bathroom and didn't say anything, neither did I.

I had no idea what was going on with her at the moment, but I knew better than to ask. All I said to her was "Goodnight, Harley," as she climbed into bed.

"Goodnight, Claire." She said nothing else as she turned the light off.

I knew that Harley was most likely thinking of Cassie, and just wanted some form of release, but I meant it when I said I couldn't lose another sister. I grew up with Harley and Violet just as much as I had Cassie, we fought like sisters, we made up like sisters, but most importantly we loved each other like sisters. I would have missed either one of them just as much as I miss Cassie.

I looked over my shoulder. Harley was still awake, staring at the ceiling. I turned back around. I let her be with her thoughts.

The next morning Violet woke us up at six.

"Come on, wake up," she said, poking me in the shoulder. I tried to flutter my eyelids open, but they felt heavy.

"Ugg, why would you wake us up this early?" I whined sitting up.

Harley was already up. I looked at her, she showed no resemblance to last night. I wondered what she was thinking.

"We're going to Disneyland," Harley said.

At that Violet had a gigantic smile. I couldn't help but smile myself, forgetting last night in the process.

"Well then hurry up and get ready," Violet said, throwing a pillow at me.

"Okay." I said getting up.

I rushed to the bathroom and got ready.

"The hotel has a tram that'll take us there," Harley said, closing the hotel door. We had all finished getting ready and were now leaving the hotel.

By the time we got on the tram it was 7.25. Once we got to the park we went through security. We finally got through right at eight, which was when the park opened. We had the choice of Disneyland or California Adventure, we all agreed on Disneyland, since it was so iconic.

The first thing we saw after going through the ticket check was a huge bush that said Disneyland, with two entrances. We went through one to reveal main street.

"I can't believe we're here," Violet squealed.

She looked like a kid, in awe of the place. Harley laughed. "Glad you like it so much," Harley said.

My stomach growled.

"Looks like it's time for breakfast," Harley said with a laugh. We decided to get cream cheese pretzels for breakfast, which were amazing, then decided to start in the back of the park and work our way to the front. The most back of the park was *Star Wars* themed. It was pretty cool, especially to Violet. She was a total nerd. It reminded me of Brandon.

He didn't look like a nerd, but he totally was. When he and Cassie first started dating she told him that she'd never seen *Star Wars*, and they spent a whole day watching all of them. She thought that they were just okay, but still would rewatch them with him every once in a while.

Even though he was a total nerd, he was actually quite athletic.

He played football, and was actually quite good. I guess that's why Cassie originally started dating him: she was really good at soccer, so she always liked to date guys she could talk about sports with. She had dated guys before, but she really fell head over heels for Brandon, and it's safe to say that he did the same for her. They had such a strong bond, even when they fought, and believe me they did. My sister can be very stubborn, but like the rest of us, he always loved her. At least they had each other when they died.

"Hello, Earth to Claire." I looked up to see Harley waving her hand in front of my face. I shook my head.

"Sorry. Still getting used to the time change," I said, which wasn't entirely a lie. I was exhausted. Jetlag is a bitch.

We were in line for the ride where you get to go inside the Millennium Falcon. It was an extremely long line, but it was better than nothing. After an hour and a half of waiting in line we finally got to go on the ride, which was totally worth it.

When we got off we headed over to a gift shop there, and me and Violet got droids, while Harley got a lightsaber, which was red. When we were walking out Violet decided to put her droid on the ground, which was a horrible idea.

As we were walking a kid, who looked to be about five, saw the droid and started sprinting towards it at full speed. Apparently the kid must have thought it was a soccer ball, because after running at it he proceeded to kick it. I looked over at Violet who looked like she watched someone die. Harley started to laugh.

"Oh my gosh, I'm so sorry. Let me pay for it." I looked up to the child's mother rushing towards us. I looked behind her to see a man, most likely her husband, carrying a baby. They both looked a bit stressed and worn.

"It's okay. He's just a little one, we totally understand," I assured them.

Harley was still laughing. Violet was looking sadly at her droid. She looked heartbroken. "Oh thank you. I am so sorry," the mother said, grabbing the kid.

"It's okay," I said.

They walked off and seemed to be having a pep talk with the kid. I turned around to see Harley hunched over still laughing. Violet picked up her droid, her eyes watery.

"Om my gosh, that made my day," Harley said standing up. Violet looked up, about to cry.

"I'm sure the droid is fine," I said, trying to calm her down. Violet didn't say anything, she just looked back down at it.

"Come on, let's take it back to the shop," Harley said between giggles. Violet shot her a dirty look.

"It's not funny." She sniffled. Harley was still giggling.

Thankfully the droid was okay, the workers at the shop said that it just turned off, then they showed us how to turn it back on in case it ever happened again. Violet decided to carry the droid in the bag the rest of the day.

I thought it was a smart choice.

We decided to go to the Blue Bayou restaurant for lunch which was amazing. We spent the whole day walking around Disneyland, and going on rides. Thankfully the roller coasters here were a lot less scary, so Violet agreed to go on them.

For dinner we backtracked to the Red Rose Tavern. Then for dessert we went to the Golden Horseshoe. It was the opposite way we were going, but they had amazing root beer floats and ice cream. I loved ice cream, but I couldn't pass up their root beer float. I looked outside from where I was sitting inside the Golden Horseshoe. It was getting dark, the fireworks would most likely start soon. I looked over at Violet who was smiling while drinking her root beer float.

"That good?" I asked. She smiled and nodded.

"Yeah, I remember for my tenth birthday my parents took me here; it was a few months before my dad passed. My mom felt a bit sick one of the nights, so it was just me and my dad. We came in here and we both got giant root beer floats. We sat right over there," she said pointing to a table near the middle of the room.

I smiled at her.

"They are pretty damn good," I said.

She smiled, then turned to look at the table she pointed to. Violet had lost her dad when she was ten, so it was just her and her mom. It was so hard on her, I remember when it happened she had a horrible time. She was super close with her dad, so it shattered her heart when he died. I could only imagine how she felt, she lost a father and a sister in a span of seven years. I grabbed her hand and gave it a squeeze.

"Thank you," she said. I gave her a smile.

Harley must have picked up the sad vibe, so she took it into her hands to lighten the mood. "How's the droid?" Harley asked.

Violet shot her another dirty look.

"Oh come on, you know it was a little funny. The kid thought it was a soccer ball," Harley said, starting to giggle.

Violet smiled, then started to snicker. "See," Harley said.

I started to laugh too.

"Okay now that I look back on it, it is a bit funny," Violet admitted between laughs.

"It was hilarious," Harley said.

I started to laugh.

"It was pretty funny," I agreed. BOOM.

I looked back outside to see a firework go off. "I guess the show is starting," I said.

"Let's go watch," Violet said, getting up.

"I have a better idea," Harley said with a smirk.

"I don't know about this one, Harls," I said.

We were in line for Thunder Mountain.

"Trust me, the wait time is like ten minutes, plus we'll be able to see the fireworks from the ride," Harley said.

Sure enough ten minutes later we were on the ride, we weren't really able to get the greatest view of the fireworks, but it was still a ton of fun, and it was only a ten minute wait. We went on rides for the rest of the time we were there, and since it was during the show, most ride lines were about ten to fifteen minutes.

We stayed until the park closed. It was a bit sad leaving, but at least we got to go. On the tram there were a few families with little kids, and every single one of them was asleep in their parents' arms, or exhausted. I smiled remembering the times where I would spend a whole day playing with Cassie, Harley, and Violet. I feel like that was yesterday.

It's funny how fast time goes by when you're having fun, you don't even realize that you're creating a core memory. I looked over at Violet, who seemed just as tired as the kids, then at Harley who seemed quite awake. I looked up and before I knew it we were back at the hotel. As I got off the bus I thought about all of the core memories we made.

Harley

"Cassie!" I yelled.

I was back in a field right next to the freeway. Cassie was standing right in front of me. "Hey, Harls, don't worry I'm just going for a drive," she said.

All of a sudden she was in her car.

"Cassie no! Don't get in the car!" I screamed.

I was about to run after her, but hit a clear wall. I hit the wall repeatedly. "NOOO!" I screamed.

"Bye, Harls," she said as her car crashed into an electrical box.

"CASSIE!" I screamed, as the car exploded.

I woke up with sweat running down my face. I was panting like crazy. *I'm okay, it was just a dream*, I told myself. I had been having nightmares like this almost every night since we left Ohio. Most nights I would just sneak down to the gym in our hotel, but last night Claire caught me.

I looked over to make sure she was soundly asleep, then slipped on a tank top, and a pair of leggings. As I was about to leave I thought back to last night and the look she gave me. I felt awful for worrying her, but I needed to run. I looked over to make sure one last time that she was asleep before I left. She was. I reached for the handle, but something inside me made me stop. I remembered what she had said to me.

"I already lost one sister."

It rang inside my head for a minute.

I walked back to where I left my pajamas, and slipped them back on. I couldn't bear knowing that I worried her that much. She already lost Cassie, and in a lot of ways me and Cassie were very similar, we both had risk-taking personalities. I'm sure Claire worried about her when she was still alive, but now I could only imagine what she must have thought when she found out that I tried to slip out of our safe hotel room at odd hours, especially when we're far from home.

I got back into bed. My head kept replaying the nightmare over and over again until finally after hours I was able to clear my mind and fall asleep.

Sadly the peaceful sleep didn't last very long. Before I knew it I had Violet shaking me awake. I really did not want to get up.

"I'm going to get coffee from downstairs since someone does not want to wake up," Violet said, throwing on a hoodie over her pajamas.

"Okay," Claire murmured.

We both knew that we wouldn't have to ask Violet to get us something too, she would get us coffee, it was just how we were. I heard the door lock click back, then decided to close my eyes, hoping for some sleep.

"I saw you last night," Claire said. "Thank you," she said after pausing.

"Huh," was all I said.

"I heard you wake up too. Try doing something before you go to bed, like reading or working out, it helps with nightmares."

"Okay," I said.

"But if you're going to work out, please do it at a decent time like nine o'clock," Claire asked.

"Okay." I didn't say any more, I just went back to sleep, and she did the same.

I knew she was worried, and I couldn't blame her for it. She had just lost a sister, and here I am sneaking out in the middle of the night.

We stayed quiet.

About ten minutes later Violet came back carrying three cups of coffee. She set it down on a night table next to where I was sleeping.

"You should get up," Violet said, nudging me.

I looked at the time, it was already ten o'clock. I had no idea that it was already ten o'clock. Part of me considered just sleeping today and driving later tonight, but I knew that it would take forever if we did that.

"Okay," I said, finally getting up.

"So what's the plan?" Violet asked. I sat up and stretched.

"We're driving to the beach at Santa Monica, then driving to Arizona," I said after stretching. "But first I have to drink that coffee." I reached over and grabbed the cup.

"If you want I can drive," Claire offered.

"No," Violet said a little too fast.

I love Claire, but she is an awful driver. "I got it, but thanks," I said.

I got up.

"I guess we should get going." I sighed. I did not want to get out of bed.

By the time we got to Santa Monica it was about twelve. We had stopped for lunch on the way at In-N-Out again. We couldn't help but get one last burger from there. They were amazing after all.

The beach was beautiful, but sadly filled with people. Violet and Claire set out to sunbathe, while I judged them for not wanting to get in the water.

"You guys aren't going to go in the water?" I complained.

Claire took one disgusted look at the water, turned to me and simply said, "No."

"Why not?" I whined.

"I don't do the ocean," she said, not opening her eyes.

"Yeah, there are all kinds of weird and creepy creatures," Violet agreed. I rolled my eyes.

"You are more than welcome to go in if you want, Harls," Claire said, still not opening her eyes. I pointed my chin up and spun around.

"Maybe I will," I said, walking towards the water.

I didn't understand why they were so disgusted, it's just salty water. I ran in until I was a little higher than waist deep, and immediately regretted it. It was freezing. I yelped and sprinted out of the water as fast as I could. I ran back to Claire and Violet and grabbed a towel.

"What's wrong, I thought it was just water?" Claire said, smirking. I threw my wet towel and smiled at her.

"Feel for yourself," I said laughing. Claire yelped as Violet let out a giggle.

"It was freezing," I said, sitting down on the warm sand.

"Told you," Claire boasted.

I rolled my eyes, and spread out on the sand, lying down. It was warm, like being on a huge blanket. After about twenty minutes I drifted asleep. When I woke up about thirty minutes had passed. I had sand all over my body, and a handful in my hair, but at least I was warm. I looked over, Claire was also asleep, and Violet was reading. I walked over and poked Claire in the ribs. "Hey!" she said, jolting up.

"I'm bored, you guys wanna play a game?" I asked.

"What kind of game?" Violet asked, pulling her attention away from the book. I smiled as I pulled out a volleyball from the bag I took with me.

We set up the portable net I brought, which was meant for badminton, but we needed an even number for that. Technically we did for volleyball too, but it was easier to get tag-teamed in volleyball than in badminton. It was me against Claire and Violet since I had the most athletic background.

Claire was somewhat athletic, and Violet... definitely tried her best. I, on the other hand, had grown up playing sports, usually with Cassie. I tried them all at least once, and played as many sports as I could in school, but I only played club soccer, like Cassie. Claire tried tennis in middle school, and did a season on JV, but stopped. Violet did dance and soccer when she was five, along with T-ball. Sadly she stopped shortly due to hatred of sports.

I grabbed the ball and jump served. Claire tried to hit the ball but it ended up going sideways at Violet who proceeded to scream and move out of the way.

"Sorry," Claire said, helping Violet up.

I made the decision to not jump serve any more. Claire threw the ball back to me, which I served under hand, and Claire hit the ball over the net. I ended up scoring again anyway, but let Claire serve. Eventually both Claire and Violet somewhat got the hang of it to where we could have rallies. Even though they weren't exactly going pro, they seemed to be having fun.

When Cassie was still alive we would usually play two v two, and me and Cassie were never on the same team to keep it fair. Most of the time it would end up just being me against Cassie, with very little help. Since she was gone, I now realized how much we carried our teams.

We didn't keep score today, but if I had to guess, I would say that I won by a lot. "That was fun," Violet said, as we put the net away.

I laughed.

"Maybe you should go out for school," I said.

"Not that much fun," Violet said with a laugh.

We went back to our spot, and sat back down and laughed and talked. Violet took some pictures of the beach and of us.

"We should probably get going," I said, checking the time. It was almost four thirty.

"You're probably right," Claire said, checking the time herself.

It felt as if we had only been there twenty minutes. I always envied people who lived at the beach. Ohio is not known for its amazing weather.

We packed up all of the stuff we brought and went back to the car. Our luggage was in the car: we packed it before we left the hotel, so that way we could leave straight for the beach. By the time we were back in LA it was five thirty. We drove through on our way to Arizona. After we were through LA we decided to stop for dinner. We stopped at a burger place called The Habit.

Violet got a grilled cheese, Claire got a chicken sandwich, and I got a burger. It was delicious. I looked over at Violet who then dipped her grilled cheese in ranch. I cringed, grilled cheese did not belong in ranch.

"That is gross," I said. Violet laughed.

"It's a lot better than it looks," she said, taking another bite of her abomination. I scrunched my face, then went back to eating.

"Can I try it?" Claire asked.

I looked at her like she was dumb.

"Of course!" Violet said, ripping off a small piece of her sandwich and dipping it in ranch. She handed it to Claire, who popped it in her mouth.

"Not bad," Claire said. I cringed again.

"You guys are disgusting," I said, taking a bite of my burger. They both laughed. I laughed a bit too.

I will never understand what possessed them to eat that.

As soon as we finished eating we got back on the road. As usual the music was blaring, and the laughter and karaoke was loud. As tired as I was, I didn't mind the drive. It was kind of nice. When we finally got there it was midnight. We were in Scottsdale, Arizona. We checked into our hotel, and took all of our luggage to our room.

I plopped onto the bed, once inside our room.

"Just wait until you guys see what I have planned," I said, smiling.

Claire and Violet continuously asked me to tell them the plan for the next three days, but I just smiled. I think they are going to love what I have in store. I got ready for bed, and went to sleep, and was sweetly surprised with no nightmares.

Violet

I woke up at around eight, which was a bit late for me. I got up and nudged Claire. "What?" she grumbled, her face still buried in the pillow.

"It's morning," I said, nudging her again.

"Ugg," she groaned and rolled over.

She did not look happy.

"I need coffee," she whined.

"We'll get you some coffee," I promised. "Okay."

She looked over at Harley who was still asleep.

"What do you think she has planned for us?" she asked curiously.

"I have no idea," I admitted.

To be completely honest, I really had no idea.

"I guess we'll find out shortly," I said as I got up.

I walked over to Harley and gently poked her in the shoulder.

"Just five more minutes," she whined, turning her head into the pillow.

"Come on, it's time." She didn't move. I knew exactly what she was waiting for. I rolled my eyes. "I'll get you coffee," I said.

Immediately she turned around. "Fine," she said sitting up.

"So will you tell us what we're doing now?" I asked. She laughed.

"Hold on," she said, taking a big stretch.

She got up, and went to her suitcase. She pulled out three Dodger shirts. I was utterly confused. "I thought that the Dodgers played in LA," I said.

"They do, but it's spring training," Harley said, tossing me and Claire each our own shirt.

I was never really into sports, but I enjoy watching them at times. I have no idea what's going on half the time, but that's why I usually go with people like Harley. I didn't care for baseball, but it was one of Harley's favorite sports to watch, and since she was a Dodger fan, along with Cassie, me and Claire, I always rooted for them.

I remembered when Cassie put spring training on the list, even I thought it sounded cool to see so many teams all in one area.

"You didn't even hear the best part," Harley said.

"Well what is it then?" Claire asked.

"We have not only one, but two games to go to," Harley said, grinning from ear to ear.

I could tell she was excited. I was too. Even though I wasn't super into baseball, it still looked like a ton of fun to watch.

"Well let's go then," Claire said, standing up.

As I got ready I threw on the Dodger shirt Cassie got me. I never understood why Cassie and Harley were Dodger fans since we lived in Ohio, but never asked them. It could be because they also happen to be Chris Taylor fans.

We left at around nine, and made a pit stop for coffee as promised. When we got to the field it was unreal. It was a lot smaller than their usual stadiums, but still a decent size. I looked around in awe as the players warmed up.

It was unreal, the Dodgers shared a spring training stadium with the Rockies, so each team had half the stadium dedicated to them. In the back of the stadium, behind right center, there was a fan store. Since we were a bit early we decided to take a look at the fan store. We all got matching tank tops that said *Cactus League* on them, which according to Harley, is the name of the spring training league, because apparently there's more than one.

We found our seats, which were behind left field. Thankfully it was about eighty degrees outside, the weather was beautiful.

"This is perfect baseball weather," Harley said, as we sat down.

Me and Claire looked at each other and shrugged. We enjoyed watching sports at times, but were pretty clueless. I felt bad that Harley didn't have anyone to talk baseball with at the moment. I remember her and Cassie would talk about sports for hours.

"I just know that it's a whole lot better than Ohio," Claire said, with a shrug.

Harley rolled her eyes, but was unable to hide the smile forming on her face. I smiled too, it was pretty hard not to.

A bit later the game began. We were up one to nothing by the third inning. Harley commented on the game for me and Claire so we had an idea of what was going on. I tried to keep up, but only understood bits and pieces of it.

Around the fifth inning my stomach growled. I laughed a bit along with Claire and Harley. "Don't worry, the seventh inning stretch is soon," Claire said.

"No, this is actually the perfect time to go get food. It'll get crowded during the seventh inning stretch," Harley said, getting up.

"You're the expert," Claire agreed, also getting up.

We went to the concession stands and got snacks. I got a pretzel, Harley got nachos, and Claire got ice cream, which came in a little Dodger hat.

"Shit, I almost forgot!" Harley said about a minute after we sat down.

"What?" Claire asked, looking over at her.

Harley set her food down and reached in her bag. She pulled out her old glove. I was a bit confused.

"Are you gonna go sub in?" Claire asked. Harley rolled her eyes.

"In case they hit a home run," Harley explained.

"The chances of that happening at exactly where we're sitting is like a hundred to one," Claire said.

"You never know. Would you rather get hit with the ball?" Harley said.

"Fair enough, but home run or not you better not let me get hit," Claire said.

"Please, I could catch a ball in my sleep," Harley said with a grin.

"You better," Claire said.

I laughed and went back to eating. The pretzel was amazing, and according to Harley and Claire their food was also amazing. When the seventh inning stretch did finally come, all three of us sang along to "Take Me Out to the Ball Game" and relaxed until the short-lived break was over.

Before I knew it it was the bottom of the ninth, the game was tied. Harley was on the edge of her seat.

I always thought that it was so funny that some people got so invested in a game they weren't even playing. Harley's muscles loosened up just a tiny amount, most people wouldn't have even seen it, as the next batter walked up to the plate.

"Is he good?" I asked.

"Yes, he's my favorite batter on the lineup," Harley said.

I looked up at the scoreboard which read, Mookie Betts. The scoreboard also happened to read two outs. The first pitch was a strike, which caused Harley to tense up even more next to me. The pitch after that was a ball. Harley looked like she was about to explode.

BAM!

He hit the ball, and everyone in the stands jumped up. I was so focused that he hit the ball, that it took me a minute to realize where he hit it.

Directly at us.

I looked over just in time to see Harley jump up and make an impressive catch. She looked wide eyed at the ball, as if she was still processing what had just happened. Me and Claire were also shocked, then started jumping up and down.

"YEAH, HARLEY!" Claire screamed.

"Told you I could catch it," she said, smirking, trying to stay cool.

Claire rolled her eyes and smiled. The little girl sitting behind us looked in awe. Harley must have seen this because she turned and looked at the child. She smiled.

"Here," Harley said, handing her the home run ball. "Just don't forget to do the same for the next girl."

The girl looked awestruck. Her parents tried to give the ball back but Harley just waved them off.

"One of my friends that really wanted to be here couldn't make it, and if she were here she would want me to," Harley explained.

"Thank you so much. I hope your friend makes it to the next game," the girl's mother said. Harley smiled softly.

"Me too," Harley said under her breath.

Harley turned around before we could talk to her about the events that just unfolded before us. "I got us tickets to a Cubs game too. We better go, their stadium is a bit further," Harley said, putting her glove back in her bag.

The car ride to the next field was silent for the most part. It wasn't until we were five minutes from the stadium until I got the courage to try and start a conversation.

"That girl was adorable," I said, trying to start any form of small talk I could get.

"Yeah," Harley agreed.

It was silent for a minute. Out of the blue Claire asked a question, that by the looks of it she couldn't hold in much longer.

"Why did you give it to her?" she blurted.

Harley smiled, not a normal smile, but a soft one, one I never really saw on her.

"Cassie always complained about the adults at baseball games that fought over foul balls, when they should let the little ones have them. She told me that any baseball game she went to she would always give whatever she caught to the kids," she explained, all while wearing the soft smile upon her face.

After hearing her reasoning, I grew a soft smile of my own, remembering that Cassie was not only fun, but kind. We pulled up to the stadium all thinking about her. Even though someone dies, the things they do never die.

When we walked into the stadium it was just as breathtaking as the last. We found our seats behind left field again. Once again we decided to get up in the fifth inning. We weren't hungry this time, but had to pee, so we made our way to the bathroom. As expected the line was very long.

We made it back to our seats within the inning. Sadly there was no home run hit directly to us this game, so Claire's odds were only "slightly" off as she said. At least Harley's glove came in handy once today. The second game was almost as fun as the last… almost. Harley was a lot more relaxed this game since the Dodgers weren't playing.

She said that she didn't really dislike or like the two teams playing at the moment, so she couldn't care less who won. Those two teams were the Cubs, obviously, and the Angels. She still tried to explain to me and Claire as the game went on, and once again I failed to keep up the entire time.

It was slightly easier than the first game to somewhat understand, though, but sadly it didn't matter, because I still was pretty confused in the end. The Angels ended up winning 5–2. I didn't realize until we were walking back to the car how tiring baseball games are, and that's just watching.

"Can we get McDonalds?" Claire asked, who also appeared to be tired.

"That sounds amazing right now," I agreed from the back seat.

"Agreed," Harley said from the driver's seat.

I was practically drooling just thinking about fries. When we pulled up to the parking lot I had to drag myself to the restaurant. Claire looked to be doing the same, while Harley, on the other hand, looked fine. I never understood how she and Cassie used to stay up so late. We got our food and sat down. The only thing keeping me awake at this point was the food set in front of me.

"You guys already tired?" Harley asked with a smirk.

"Yes," I groaned, putting my head on the table.

"Too bad, there's a club not too far from here," Harley said.

I groaned without picking my head up. Claire joined me. Harley let out a laugh. "I'm kidding," Harley assured us.

I picked my head off the table, which was surprisingly comfy. "Cassie would've partied all night with me," Harley said.

Her soft smile returned, but this time there was a hint of

longing in it. "Yeah, we're not Cassie," Claire said, matching her smile.

I joined them too. It was hard not to miss someone when everything reminds you of them. We once again returned to silence. I didn't bother trying to break it this time; I didn't have the energy, or will. Claire must have shared those feelings, because she stayed quiet too.

Once we finished up, we went back to the hotel and went to bed without a word. It was too painful. It was like a wound that never really healed, it was a cut, and every time it finally starts to close, something opens it back up again. Every time my mind cleared, in the very back of it, Cassie was there, whether it was singing along in the car to a song, talking about sports, partying, or just being her, she was always there.

I couldn't help but miss her, she lived in my head, along with everybody else's. How were we just supposed to forget her when she was so amazing? Maybe it would just be easier to forget people when they die, like they die from everyone's mind along with their body.

I don't think Cassie will ever exactly have that second death, or at least not for a long time. She affected too many people in a positive way to truly be forgotten. Maybe that's one of the reasons we die, to be remembered for what we did, instead of who we are. It's weird to think that everyone dies; I know I never thought of it until I lost Cassie.

Everyone we know has to end at some point, but we don't know when. It's a clock ticking down to a time that only fate knows. I guess that's why Cassie lived her life so full and happy, maybe she had this thought herself. Maybe she just didn't want to have that many regrets when fate stopped her clock. That's one of the reasons she was so loved, and now missed, because she didn't let fate dictate how she would be remembered, she chose her own legacy.

I fell asleep that night to the memories of her legacy, because in death, that's all we can leave to our loved ones for comfort.

Claire

I have never been considered a "sports person". It's not who I am, but I would be lying if I said that I didn't love every minute of the two games yesterday. As soon as I saw the girl sitting behind us after Harley caught that ball, I knew what would happen. I was there when Cassie talked about it.

I smiled at the thought.

My sister just couldn't help herself, always having to put someone first. I wonder if the pressure ever got to her. She was amazing at soccer, pressure, got decent grades, pressure, for the last two years was at work all of the time, pressure, and still tried to be an amazing person and look out for everyone, pressure. To this day I still have no idea how she did it.

BEEP! BEEP! BEEP!

The alarm went off, but my eyes were already open. Violet actually slept longer than me, which is a rare sight. She was exhausted after the games yesterday. I don't blame her; I was too. I sat up and looked over at Harley who slammed her hand on the alarm clock, sending out silence. I wondered if her nightmares had stopped. She never said that she had them, but I could tell.

She grabbed the pillow and put it over her head. I smiled, I was usually the one to do that. Violet got up without a single complaint. She had always been a morning person. She was about to poke me when I turned around, startled, she stopped.

"You scared me," she said. "You're up early, before me. Are you okay?" she said, with a growing concern on her face.

"I'm fine," I assured her, as a smile grew on my face.

I sat up and took a big morning stretch. I wasn't a morning person, but I did enjoy the stretch. Violet got up and walked over to Harley and gently tapped her.

"Just five more minutes," she mumbled from under her pillow.

I agreed with her, I hadn't realized my exhaustion this morning until she had said something. "We can get coffee again," Violet said.

Harley stopped for a moment, causing me to think that she fell back asleep, but then responded, "Fine."

This also made me realize that I would also favor coffee at the moment.

Harley finally got up, which made me get up. We left the hotel, then went to breakfast at Starbucks.

We sat down at a table after getting our coffee and food. As the rest of the trip I was curious in matters of the daily agenda. I had a small amount of OCD so I liked to know when things were happening, and what was happening. It complicated the trip a bit, but didn't ruin it, so I always held my tongue until the next day.

"What's the plan?" I asked.

"Shopping," Harley said, with a smile. Violet grinned.

"I think that's a great idea," Violet said, with a huge smile. I laughed along with Harley.

"Least I'll understand what's going on this time," I said, with a laugh.

We left and got to the mall around ten. It was huge. We walked in, like every mall there was a long wall lined with stores. It was two stories, which meant twice as many stores. I didn't have to look to know that Violet was extremely happy.

"Where to first?" I asked.

"I say… H&M," Violet said grinning.

Harley chuckled.

"Sounds like a plan," Harley said.

We made our way over to H&M. As always the store was filled with cute clothes. We made our way through the store trying on all of the clothes we found cute. Violet had always loved shopping, and who doesn't? Me and her would go to the mall together most weekends when Harley and Cassie had practice.

I looked over at Harley, who was looking at a bright red tank top. She would most likely pair it with black jean shorts if she bought it. I remember one night Cassie told Harley that she should wear red more, and I can see why, it suits her really well. It looked great with her long black hair.

I don't know if even Harley has noticed, but since her death she has worn more red. It might just be a coincidence, I mean I don't think she has even noticed. I guess that's the funny thing about the mind, it does things that we don't even realize.

I looked over to Violet, who of course had pastel-colored clothes. She rarely wore dark clothes, she was always dressed in lighter colors. It was funny to me, it matched her bubbly personality. It's funny how much you can tell about someone just based on how they dress. She picked a violet-colored sweater, which was a bit ironic. It was ironic that her name doubled as her favorite color.

We made our way through the store, picking up cute finds here and there. When we did try them on, we ended up only getting a few things.

"Does this make my ass look flat?" Harley asked, looking at the shorts she was trying on. I rolled my eyes.

"Is that the thing that you should really be concerned about?" I asked.

"Duh," Harley said. I couldn't help but smile.

"How else are you supposed to attract the male species?" Harley said in a nature documentary voice.

"Boobs," I said with a shrug.

Harley laughed and threw a shirt on the ground at me. I started laughing at my own joke. I forgot how funny I can be sometimes.

"Or you could just wear clothes that YOU think are cute, and not for someone else," Violet said, folding the clothes she was going to put back.

"You could, but where's the fun in that?" Harley said. For the third time in this conversation, I rolled my eyes.

"If you keep rolling them they're gonna get stuck up there," Harley said, putting her own clothes back on.

I waited for her to make eye contact with me, then rolled my eyes. "Whatever, Mom," I said super sarcastically.

We all laughed.

"Your poor mother. She had to raise Cassie's craziness, and your attitude," Harley said, still laughing.

"Who? Me?" I said, with a fake gasp. "Never. I am such an angel, I have no idea what you're talking about," I said through a smirk. Harley rolled her eyes with a smile. "Careful, they'll get stuck," I said, mimicking her from moments before.

"Whatever, Mom," she said, mimicking me right back.

I let out a laugh. We gathered the clothes we were going to buy and checked out. We made our way to the next store which was Guess. The store was super cute, but not exactly my style. It was a bit too edgy for me. Violet appeared to share the opinion, but it was perfect for Harley.

Harley found an off the shoulder black leather dress that was tight fitting, and a bit too short for my taste. She also found some black ankle boots to go with it.

"For the next club," she teased, as she checked out.

"Your butt is going to be hanging out of it," I said.

"Like I said, how else are you supposed to attract the male species?" she said, biting back a laugh.

I lightly smacked her in the arm. The cashier looked extremely uncomfortable. He was a scrawny boy, who looked to be about the same age as us. His cheeks were bright red. "Sorry," I said to the boy. "She can be a bit crazy," I said, pointing to Harley.

Harley acted fake offended and put her hand over her heart. "Uncalled for," she said.

The boy let out an awkward laugh, clearly not knowing what to say. Well, I tried.

Out of the corner of his eye, he seemed to be looking at Violet. He blushed even harder. Interesting.

I forced myself not to smile.

Violet was very awkward around guys, but she was extremely pretty, and could probably get a cute guy with ease, but she was always too focused on school.

"I think you scared the poor kid," I whispered to Harley, as we walked out of the store.

"He seemed a bit too distracted for that," Harley said, nudging Violet. Her cheeks turned a bright pink.

"I... uh... he probably wasn't looking at me," Violet sputtered, practically tripping over her words.

Like I said, awkward.

"Maybe you should borrow the dress," Harley said. Violet let out an awkward laugh.

"I think I'll pass," she said, smiling. Harley shrugged.

"Worth a try."

My stomach growled, causing Violet to giggle. "I could go for some food though," Violet said.

I checked the time on my phone, it was already twelve thirty. "My stomach agrees," I said.

We walked to the food court and found a very healthy and nutritious lunch. "Can I get a pizza pretzel?" I asked the cashier at Wetzel's.

"Sure thing," she said, rigging me up. We got our food, and found a table.

"I don't know if I'll be able to fit into the dress after this," Harley said between bites of her pretzel.

"You are very dramatic," I said.

Harley laughed. I can't remember the last time I had Wetzel's, but I did remember how good it was, and this time was no different. Harley and Cassie also seemed to enjoy it.

"That was amazing," I said, as I finished my pretzel.

"No kidding," Harley agreed.

I checked the time, to discover that it was one o'clock.

"What store is in store for us?" I said, laughing at my own joke.

Harley cringed, while Violet laughed. Violet always appreciated my dad jokes and puns. "Respectfully, shut up," Harley said.

Harley did not appreciate them as much.

"You're just mad that I'm funnier than you," I said, laughing. It was Harley's turn to roll her eyes.

"You are stupid, and to answer your question there's a Tilly's if you two are good with that," Harley replied.

"Sounds good," I said.

We threw our trash away, and made our way to Tilly's. We always had fun shopping at Tilly's because it had something for all of our styles. We tended to go there a lot when it was the four of us.

When we got there I immediately found something that was to die for. It was overalls. Harley and Violet seemed to be pleased with what they found too. Violet came back with a white skirt, and a pastel blue shirt, while Harley appeared with a plaid button up, and a black crop top. I could already see the clothes on both of them.

"Those are cute," Harley said, looking at the overalls.

"Thanks." I beamed.

We made our way over to the fitting rooms. Luckily everything fit, so we went to check out then left. We walked around the mall for about another hour, then decided to head back to the hotel for some much needed rest.

It was two forty-five when we got to the car. I was starting to vividly feel the exhaustion from the past few days. I yawned as I made my way to the passenger seat. I nearly fell asleep as we drove away from the mall.

We got back to the hotel around three o'clock, then we unloaded our shopping bags from the trunk and made our way to our room. When we finally got to the room I dropped my shopping bags, and practically collapsed on the bed.

"You okay?" Violet asked.

"Yeah," I mumbled, my face buried in the blanket.

"Okay, good," Violet said, falling next to me.

Harley shortly followed. Before I knew it I was passed out. I was so tired that I didn't even dream. I just slept, my mind blank, as dark as a black hole.

I felt someone nudge me, most likely Violet. I pulled my pillow over my head. "Why?" I complained from under my pillow.

I felt another gentle nudge.

"It's almost four o'clock," Violet said softly.

"Ugg," I said, not moving.

"We still have another thing planned," Violet said.

I thought about just lying there while Violet and Harley went on and did the thing planned, but then thought of my sister. She would drag me out of bed, and make me go and have the time of my life. I smiled at the thought.

I forced myself to sit up, and immediately regretted it. I wanted so badly to just fall back down and sleep, but forced myself to stay up. Violet walked over to Harley and did the same to her as she did me. Harley had a similar response, but eventually woke up.

At least I wasn't the only one.

"So what is so important that I had to awake?" I asked, still sitting down.

"We're going to downtown Scottsdale," Harley said, stretching.

"It sounds so awesome," Violet said, bouncing in place.

Our hotel wasn't too far from downtown, and I could see why Violet was so excited. It looked extremely nice.

"Okay," I said, finally getting out of bed.

I walked over to the bathroom and got ready. I put on the overalls I got, with a black tight T-shirt underneath. Violet had on a peach-colored T-shirt, and light-colored, baggy jeans, while Harley had on dark blue jeans, with a navy long sleeve, that was tight fitting. We finished getting ready at five o'clock, and got to downtown at five fifteen.

It was beautiful; the streets were lined with shops, and restaurants. There were even some fairy lights in most of the area.

"Wow, it's amazing," I said as we found a parking spot.

Harley smiled.

"Yeah, just wait till dinner," Harley said.

"What type of food is it?" I asked.

"Mexican, but the place is super authentic," Harley replied, turning the car off.

I wondered how good the food would be, since we didn't really have much Mexican food in Ohio. We walked to a very cute-looking building. It was painted orange, with blue tiles on the floor.

"For three," Harley said.

"Right this way," a worker responded, leading us to our table.

She led us through a small building with tables, through a patio with cute fairy lights, also filled with tables, then finally to another small building with tables. We sat down and the worker handed us menus. Everything on the menu looked amazing.

"This place is so cool," Violet said, looking around.

"Yeah, good pick, Harls," I said.

Harley smiled proudly.

"I figured Cassie would love it, based on the website," Harley said.

I smiled, taking another look around. Cassie would love this place. My thoughts were interrupted when a server came to our table.

"What can I get you ladies to drink?" I snapped out of it and smiled at the server.

"I'll take a Shirley temple," I said, with a smile.

"Me too," Violet chimed in.

"Triple that," Harley said.

"Of course," the server said, then took off.

"So what are you guys getting?" Violet asked after the server left. I still had no idea, everything looked amazing.

"I don't know yet," I said, picking up the menu.

"Me either," Harley agreed.

"Dang, I was hoping you two would help me decide." Violet sighed.

Since we didn't have that much Mexican food in Ohio, it was really hard to decide. After thoroughly reading the menu I finally decided on a burrito. Our server came by with our drinks. "You guys ready to order?" the server asked, after setting our drinks down.

"Yes we are," I said. "I'll take a burrito with ground beef."

I know that's not exactly "authentic" but it sounds really good.

"Chicken enchilada please," Harley said.

"Of course, and for you?" the server said, looking at Violet.

"Can I get a chicken taco?" Violet asked.

"Yep, I'll get that started," the waiter said, taking our menus.

We sat and talked for a bit, filling the air with normal conversations and laughter. Our food got to us in a pretty fast time for a sit down restaurant. As expected it smelled and looked amazing. "That looks so good," I said after the server walked off.

I took a bite, and like the way it looked, it was amazing. "I wish this place was in Ohio," Violet said, between bites.

"Me too," I agreed.

After we finished eating, we paid and left.

When we got outside it was starting to get a bit dark. I looked around to see that the town was booming with people. Restaurants, stores, and bars were all crowded. I looked at Harley, who looked like she was in heaven. Violet must have seen too, because her eyes went wide at the memory of Vegas.

To be completely honest, I do not remember much of that night, all I know is that Violet had one drink, so she was babysitter.

"Please don't," Violet begged. Harley started to smirk.

"No promises," she teased. Violet's eyes went even wider. "Fine," Harley finally agreed.

A part of me was actually relieved, I actually wanted to remember tonight. We walked around for about an hour, going in shops here and there, just exploring downtown. Once it started to get truly dark, more fairy lights revealed themselves throughout downtown.

"Okay I have a surprise," Harley said. I raised my eyebrow.

"Go on," I said, curious to what the surprise was.

Harley didn't say anything, but pointed to the carriages drawn by horse. Violet smiled, and I couldn't help but do the same.

"Well then let's go," I said.

The carriages were a method of transportation downtown at night, but most just used them for fun. They were a gorgeous sight, a wooden wagon, with hay to sit on, and the side panels decorated with fairy lights strung around them, pulled by horses. I laughed, knowing that Cassie most likely put this on the bucket list for her to do with Brandon.

I forgot just how much she loved him sometimes. I always wished that I had the type of bond that they had. Maybe they died together because God believed that it would be too painful for the other.

I thought about Ms. Rebrio, I hoped she was still doing well. I may have lost a sister, but she lost a son, in my opinion both are equally horrible, but then again I don't have kids for myself, so maybe when and if I do I'll feel a bit different. That would be hard to lose a kid, a person that you made, and watched grow, and raised to make them a good person. I couldn't imagine, but then again a sibling is someone you're raised with, a built-in friend, someone you share a special type of bond with, especially if they're your twin.

"Claire, you good?" I came to, with Harley standing in front of me, both her and Violet staring at me.

"Yeah, just zoned out for a minute," I said.

I used to never zone out, but since Cassie died, I've had a lot more to think about. We got into the wagon and set off.

It was gorgeous, the town was lit up by fairy lights, and people were bustling about. It was a beautiful town.

"Did you guys ever envy them?" I asked, still looking at the town.

"What?" Violet asked.

"Brandon and Cassie. They had such a good bond. Sometimes all I wanted was someone to share a bond like that with," I said, still keeping my eyes on the sight before me.

I watched as we passed by a little boutique. "I did," Harley said, also looking at the town. "But then I grew up. I realized that some people just aren't meant for that kind of love," Harley continued.

I went quiet.

"I think you're wrong," Violet said.

We both turned to look at her.

"I believe that everyone has someone meant for them. Some people are just too scared to go for it, or some have it and take it for granted and mess it up."

Her and Harley made eye contact, almost having a second conversation through them. Violet finally looked away.

"My dad used to tell me that when you find your soulmate they're more than just someone you find attractive. They're your best friend too," Violet said, keeping her eyes on the street.

Harley was still looking at Violet. Her eyes looked electric blue in the dark lighting.

"Or maybe your dad just got lucky. Some people are just meant to be alone," Harley said, looking back to the street.

The rest of the ride was quiet.

I felt a wave of exhaustion hit me after I stepped off the wagon. The trip was really starting to take a toll on me now that the adrenaline was wearing off. It was crazy to think about all the stuff that I'd done in the past eight days. Even yesterday felt like years ago.

"You guys ready to head back?" Harley asked.

"Sounds good to me," I said, already walking to the car.

When we got back to the hotel it was already eleven thirty. The only thing that forced me to wash my face and brush my teeth was pure will. After that I threw on some shorts and a hoodie, and practically collapsed into bed. Within minutes I was out. I thought about the conversation from the carriage. I didn't really think about stuff like soulmates that often.

I didn't know which idea I really believed in either. I wanted Violet's take on it to be true, but a part of me couldn't help but wonder if I was destined to be alone. Maybe there isn't always a person meant for you. Or even worse there is and you already blew it because you couldn't work up the courage to get their number, or even talk to them.

I promised myself that next time I saw a cute guy I would go and try to talk to them at the very least, since we never really know what fate has in store.

Violet

I woke up at the sound of an alarm. I was a morning person, but not usually this early. It was four forty-five in the morning, we had a flight at eight and still needed to pack. I rubbed my eyes, getting in a stretch. Since we had an alarm I didn't have to wake up Harley and Claire.

Thank God.

They weren't getting up so I let the alarm continue to sound until one of them finally got up, forcing the other one to follow. I quickly got ready and started packing. Harley and Claire did the same with their things. We got to the airport at six, which gave us plenty of time to get checked in, go through security, and get some food. We walked in and got in line to get checked in.

Harley was still half asleep. "I need coffee," she whined.

"We still have to go through security," I said, as we walked towards the security line.

"Maybe they won't notice," Harley said.

I smiled and rolled my eyes.

"Come on, it'll take like ten minutes," I said.

Claire also still seemed to be half asleep. Apparently the security line was a bit longer than ten minutes. I felt extremely bad as we waited half an hour in line. Harley seemed to be more focused on thinking about coffee than my false promise. I still felt guilty. I made a note in my head to just get her a large.

When we finally got to the front of the line Harley and Claire took their shoes off with ease, while I was clumsily trying to untie my shoes. After we went through security, once again, Harley and Claire dealt with their shoes at light speed, while I slowly put mine on.

"Come on," Claire said.

"Sorry," I said, tying my second shoe. "My bad," I said, awkwardly standing up.

The lack of sleep was finally starting to get to me, and my lack of gracefulness did not help. A coffee did not sound bad at all.

We started walking towards our gate, looking for coffee stands along the way. We found one, and decided to get it before we continued.

Harley seemed much less grumpy, and Claire seemed to wake up a bit after we finally got some. We started off towards our gate once again. We were luckily able to find three seats next to each other. I sat down, and I don't know if it was being at an airport again, or the experiences I went through in the past few days, but it all really started to hit me.

I went to Las Vegas where I faced one of my biggest fears. I partied, well kind of, all night. I went to huge malls, and that was just Vegas. I went to LA. I went to Spring training for crying out loud. I did stuff I could never picture myself doing, yet here I am. Just thinking about it sounded crazy. I could only imagine what Mexico had in store for us.

I remember the night in Vegas, right before I rode the roller coaster. I remember Harley telling me to let go, and I told her it was hard to when you've been holding on for so long, but at some point since then I let go and didn't even realize. I laughed to myself. I did things I never even dreamed of. I remembered the promise I made with Claire back in the first airport. I somewhat actually fulfilled it.

I'm usually hard on myself, but for once I am actually proud of myself, and not ashamed to admit it. I did things I never thought I'd do, and faced fears that I never thought I'd face. I looked over at Harley and Claire, who were talking about something, and smiled. Harley must have noticed and looked over.

"What's up, Vi, everyth—"

"Thank you. Both of you, for everything," I said, cutting Harley off.

Harley and Claire both looked caught off guard. I never caught Claire off guard, considering she was my best friend.

"For what?" Claire asked, confused.

"Everything. If I've learned anything these past few weeks, I've learned that we never really know how much time we have, and we never really know how much we have with certain people. Both of you forced me to live a little this trip, and I want you to know that I'm grateful. Who knows what can happen in the next year, the next week, hell maybe even in the next second, but either way I want you two to know how much you've done for me," I said.

They both looked at me for a minute, both stunned and silent. Finally Claire looked at me, her eyes looking a bit watery, and hugged me. Harley joined in. I hugged them back. I don't know when exactly I started crying, but there were tears running down my face. Claire seemed to be having the same problem.

We didn't say anything, we didn't have to. We, like many times before in these past few weeks, knew what we were all thinking. She should be here. This was for her. I cried a bit harder, missing my old friend. It was almost funny that I, who never let loose, did more crazy stuff than her in our lifetimes.

I guess life is funny that way, it always has a plot twist.

Claire and Harley finally pulled away. Claire also had tears running down her face, Harley just looked lost in thought. She looked like a child trying to put a puzzle together with a missing piece.

We started boarding shortly after our breakdown.

We were in the middle of the plane. It was a bigger plane, so there were two rows of three on each side. Harley had window seat, and I had the aisle, with Claire in the middle. Our flight was about seven hours, so we had a chance to gather ourselves. The only problem was that I had seven hours to think.

Normally that would be a dream, but right now my mind wandered to dreadful places and thoughts. I tried to never shut out emotions, it wasn't healthy, but this whole trip my mind constantly bounced back and forth between memories of Cassie, missing Cassie, and actually having fun, and letting loose. My mind was a hurricane, constantly swirling, each time pulling me closer and closer to the eye, the thoughts I don't want to think. I tried to distract myself with some movies and books. When that failed I turned to Claire, who was half asleep.

"You up for a movie?" I asked, poking her in the arm. She turned her head to me, giving me a soft smile.

"Anytime," she said.

I returned the soft smile. The movie occupied us for about three hours of the flight. Harley slept the entirety of the movie. She finally awoke about twenty minutes after the movie ended.

"How much longer do we have?" she said through a yawn, sitting up and stretching.

"About four hours," I replied.

She put her head onto the back of her chair, and let out a frustrated sigh. "That's so long," she complained. "There better be some hot guys in Mexico."

"Are we not good enough company?" Claire asked with a smirk.

"You guys are all right," Harley teased.

We started giggling. I had a feeling that the four hours would go by much faster with these two. I ended up being right, the four hours flew by with Claire and Harley. We spent the majority of the flight watching funny movies and laughing. We had a connecting flight in Huatulco. When we landed it was about 3.25 Arizona time. Once we got off the plane we had to sprint to catch our next flight, and barely made it in time. This flight was a lot shorter than the last one, only being about one hour instead of seven. The one hour seemed to go quickly, especially compared to the seven. When we landed at our final destination, Mazunte, it was about 4.39 Arizona time, but 5.39 local time. It was so crazy to me that with an eight hour flight, there was only a one hour time difference.

I stepped off the plane, immediately hit with a wave of heat and humidity. "Well, welcome to Mexico," Harley said as she stepped off the plane.

I couldn't believe that I was in a different country, or that it was the last three days of our trip. "Let's live like there's no tomorrow," Claire said.

"I agree," I said.

Me and Claire both looked at Harley. She smiled softly. "Hell yeah," she said softly.

We all smiled, awaiting the next adventure.

"Let's find some air conditioning first," Harley said with a laugh.

Harley

Time is a funny concept. Even though it's almost always consistent, it feels different. Sometimes hours can feel like minutes, while a minute can seem an entirety. This trip felt like it'd gone by so fast, as if someone clicked fast forward. We were already at our final destination. It felt unreal thinking about it.

I shook off the thoughts, I have to focus on what is happening in the exact moment. I can't let my thoughts, or emotions drift off. I can't let myself focus on what already happened. I have to keep moving, one foot in front of the other. I can't linger on the fact that we are missing a person. It only took us about twenty minutes to get to our hotel. The exhaustion from the planes and jet lag was already starting to wear off on me since I slept so much on the plane. I couldn't say the same for Claire and Violet. They looked drained.

"I think I'm going to take a quick nap," Claire said, yawning.

She looked like she needed one, with bags under her eyes, which were barely staying open. "That sounds like a good idea," I replied, watching her yawn once again.

"I'll join," Violet mumbled, too tired to speak up.

Like Claire she had bags under her eyes, and looked exhausted. "That also sounds like a good idea," I said, nodding.

A few minutes later they were both out cold. I wanted to just drift off into peaceful, uninterrupted sleep, but I had too much on my mind. I knew that if I tried I would most likely get more nightmares, and eventually start working out, so I decided to skip the nightmare part, and got on the ground and started doing push ups. No matter how hard I tried to shut it out, my mind kept wandering.

It wandered to places that were poisoned with foul memories. Memories I once loved, but now were full of mourning. I pushed myself harder, hoping that the pain and exhaustion would override my mind, but it only enhanced it. I thought back to the first time I met Cassie. We were in kindergarten; it was at recess. I gathered a group of kids and we were playing tag. She was the only one who ever caught up to me that day.

When she was the only one who caught me I was shocked. Children have big egos, and I was about to get upset, but then I realized that we were wearing the same shoes. We began to talk about whatever children talk about, and we became best friends from that moment on. I don't remember much from kindergarten, because it was so long ago, but I'll never forget that moment. How could someone ever forget that?

The memory that once filled me with joy, brought me nothing but heartbreak and sadness, and grief in this moment. I used to smile at it, but now I cried. My arms were so tired, I physically could not push myself up, but my mind still swam with memories and thoughts, so I rolled over to my back and began doing sit ups.

My forehead dripped with sweat, which rolled into my eyes and burned. I cried from a mix of two pains. I remembered back to the first time I cried in front of Cassie. I don't cry very often, and never in front of people, but I did in front of Cassie. She was the only person I wasn't scared to cry in front of. The first time I cried in front of her was when I broke up with Rodger. I couldn't help it.

At first I felt weak and stupid, but then Cassie told me that it was going to be okay and hugged me. The next day when I saw her I joked that I was weak, and she looked at me and told me that everyone cries, and that crying does not make you weak, but shows the battles you have been through.

My abs hurt from the sit ups, but once again I kept going. I went until all of the horrid thoughts and memories were safely pushed back into the corner of my mind. I got up and went into the bathroom. I looked like a mess, sweaty, my eyes swollen and red from crying. I took a quick shower, letting the warm water pour over me and consume me and my thoughts.

It was nice to have a blank mind. I got out of the shower and put on some shorts and a tank top, and climbed into bed. I checked the time, it was almost eight o'clock. Claire and Violet looked like they weren't going to wake up anytime soon, so I allowed myself to drift into sleep.

I awoke the next day to Violet nudging me. Thankfully my mind stayed blank last night, allowing me to rest without nightmares. My eyes fluttered open to reveal Violet standing over me. She looked like she had caught up on rest, her face a bit puffy, and her blond hair a frizzy mess. I sat up as Violet opened the curtains.

Golden morning light filled the room, causing Claire to mumble, and throw a pillow over her head. Violet walked over and said something to her.

"Fine," Claire said, throwing the pillow to the end of the bed.

She sat up, her hair auburn hair was a tangled mess. I checked the time, it was 7.54. I got almost twelve hours of sleep. I stretched and got up. I was sweating a bit, apparently Mexico was a bit hotter than Ohio. I walked over to my luggage and picked out my outfit. I chose a black tank top, and jean shorts.

After I changed, I brushed my teeth and washed my face, and

threw my messy black hair in a bun. I desperately needed a haircut. My hair was down to my mid back. I laced up my black converse and waited for Claire and Violet to finish getting ready.

Claire had on a green tank top and baggy jeans, while Violet had on a pastel pink T-shirt and a white skirt. Violet's once frizzy mess of hair was now neatly resting down, and Claire had hers in a high ponytail.

"You're going to regret wearing jeans," I said as Claire walked out of the bathroom.

"What is it you always say? If it's a cute fit it's worth it," she said, throwing her pajamas into her suitcase.

I let out a laugh.

"Fair enough," I said with a shrug.

"You guys ready?" Violet squealed.

"Let's go," I said, getting up.

We walked to the village since it was so close. It was a small, but beautiful, village, with little clay houses and stores. It was right on the ocean, so I could smell the salty air as we walked along. As we were walking I accidentally bumped into a man. He looked to be about thirty, a handsome man with a defined jaw.

"Sorry," I apologized.

"Oh shit, you probably don't speak English," I realized out loud.

"Ella dice que lo siento. Mi amiga está un poco loco," Violet cut in. I forgot she took like four years of Spanish. The man let out a laugh.

"It's okay, I speak English," he said in English.

He had a thick accent, but it was still English so I wasn't complaining. "My bad," I said awkwardly rubbing my arm.

"So what brings you to Mazunte?" he asked with his thick accent.

"It's kinda a weird story but ou—"

"Vacation," I said cutting Claire off.

I really didn't want to tell this stranger our sob story.

"Awesome, if you guys ever get bored you should check out the lake. It's a few miles from here, and you have to hike a little, but the water is crystal clear, and there's a cliff to jump into it from."

"And where is it again?" I asked.

"A few miles south, it's called Lago Life. You should be able to walk there."

"Thank you so much," I said.

"Of course."

"What's your name?" I asked.

"Nico, and yours?"

"Harley."

"Nice, nice meeting you, Harley," he said, flashing me a welcoming smile.

"You too," I said as he walked off.

After he was gone I turned to Violet and Claire. "Sounds pretty cool," I said.

I really wanted to go check it out now. It sounded like something Cassie would totally be down for.

"It sounds a little sketch," Claire said.

"Yeah I don't know about this one," Violet agreed with her.

I don't blame them for not wanting to go, it does sound a little sketchy, but wasn't that the point of this trip? To do things that we wouldn't normally do. I thought back to last night and all of the painful memories. Cassie would want to do this, so I was going to. I looked at Claire, my eyes pleading.

"Please," I begged.

The one word caused something to shift in her expression. I

could tell she was thinking something very similar to what I was thinking.

"Okay," she agreed.

I smiled, relieved. Violet looked at her like she was crazy. Her eyes were wide with terror.

"Are you guys insane? We are three teenage females in a foreign country going to a random lake that a random guy told us about that happens to be in the middle of the forest," Violet outburst. She did have a point, but a gut feeling told me to go.

"I have a good feeling," I said.

"Harley, it's not worth it."

I was about to protest, but then Claire cut in for me.

"Vi, let's do it." There was a look in Claire's eyes that said a thousand other words for her. Violet has always been smart and must have been able to see the thousand other words. "Fine," finally came out of her mouth.

I smiled, full of relief and newfound excitement. "You are not going to regr—"

"Hold on, I want to make sure we're safe. I want to get breakfast here, then go back to the hotel for a little bit so that way I can do some research to make sure it's legit," Violet explained, cutting me off.

I smiled, only Violet would do research on a vacation. "That's okay with me," I agreed.

Violet nodded and forced a smile, but as always her true emotions shined through like a light under a white sheet. She had a smile, but I could see the nerves and fear in her eyes. We started to walk to get breakfast. Violet was a bit more on edge than usual, probably just wanting to fast forward time to get the research done. I just wish she would slow down and enjoy what's going on around her, but she has come out of her shell a lot on this trip, so I can't complain now.

The air here was warm and thick, like walking in a blanket. I could smell the salt as we walked along. Vendors lined the street, selling crafts, and amazing smelling food. We stopped when we found a breakfast place and got our food. I laughed a little to myself, remembering how we got Mexican food in Arizona, even though we were coming here next. I probably should have thought that one through a little more.

After we finished eating we started on our way back to the hotel. I couldn't help but admire the beauty of the small town as we walked back to the town. Eventually my mind wandered back to the poisoned thoughts from last night as I walked. Cassie would have loved this place. I can practically see her next to me bouncing up and down with excitement about the lake.

No, I told myself. *I have to push it back*. I tried to ignore my brain, but I could feel the memories, and thoughts. I couldn't let it take over. I felt a sudden wave of grief wash over me, thinking about my old friend.

All of the times and memories we shared came rushing back like a lost child to their mother. I felt weak, almost as if I was being held captive in my own mind with no control over what was happening. *Just keep walking, one foot in front of the other*, I told myself. I focused my energy on keeping one foot in front of the other the rest of the walk. I was able to push my thoughts to the corner of my mind, but I could feel them slowly starting to creep back out.

The walk back only took about ten minutes, but it felt like an eternity. When we finally got back my head started to pound. Claire, as always, seemed to pick up on it.

"Harls, you okay?" she asked, with concern painted over her

face.

"I'm fine," I lied.

She knew I was lying, and she knew that I knew what she was thinking. She looked at me, and without words her eyes almost asked me why I was, but her mouth said something else.

"Okay."

I guess being able to read people is a family trait, because Cassie was able to always do it, and Claire might not be quite as good as Cassie, but she still manages to do it.

After a long moment of looking at me Claire finally turned away. My head started to pound even harder.

"I'm going to take a cat nap," I said, taking my hair out of its bun.

"Okay, I found that the place is real, and that it's about ten minutes from here, plus a twenty minute hike, so wake up at around twelve thirty," Violet responded.

"Okay," I replied.

I checked the time, it was already ten forty-five, leaving me about an hour and forty-five minutes of rest. I closed my eyes, but I didn't sleep at first. I put all of my head into pushing back the thoughts, and finally succeeded. I slept. As expected, I got nightmares, but I was now used to them, leaving me with decent sleep. Not exactly the best, but it was something.

My alarm went off at twelve thirty as Violet had instructed me. I sat up and stretched. Claire was on her phone, and Violet was doing the homework she missed on her laptop. I hadn't even thought about school since we left.

I got up and walked into the bathroom. I looked into the mirror, and I looked like I had just woken up. My hair was a mess, and my mascara was smeared on my lower eye. I took off the mascara I had on and reapplied some, and brushed my hair out and returned it to a messy bun.

I walked back to my bag and fished through until I found what I was looking for. I smiled as I pulled them out. They were the matching bikinis I bought before the trip. I smiled to myself; Cassie would have loved these. I shook off the thought. I walked over to Claire smiling. She looked at my hand, and frowned.

"No," she simply said.

"Yes," I said smiling as I tossed hers.

"Don't worry I made sure to keep them decently modest," I assured her as I walked over to give Violet hers.

I threw Violet's at her and walked off before she could protest.

"Just put them on under your clothes. We are going swimming after all," I yelled out as I walked into the bathroom.

After I was done changing I came out of the bathroom with the bikini underneath my clothes. Claire had exchanged her jeans with jean shorts. I put on boots for hiking instead of my converse.

"You guys ready?" I asked, on edge with nerves.

I was so excited, my mind had drifted back to the positive, for now at least. "Yep," Claire replied.

Violet still looked tense, her eyes still wide, and her shoulders and neck in an awkward position. "Violet, what else did your research say?" I asked, lacing up my boots.

"That it's a gorgeous place, and many tourists love it," Violet said, not sounding fully convinced. I offered her a weak smile. I knew she was trying.

"I'll get you fast food when we get back home," I said with a weak smile. That pushed a smile out of her.

"Fine, but can you wait until my cheat day? I'm still trying to work off Vegas," she replied.

"You can be so boring sometimes."

"Hey," she said, throwing a pillow at me. The three of us erupted in laughter.

"Come on," I said, getting up. "The hike will help you 'burn off Vegas'," I continued, putting air quotes around, burn off Vegas. Violet rolled her eyes, but failed to hide the smile across her face. When we got outside the hotel, we started our walk to the place. As before the air was salty, leaving, in my opinion, an amazing smell. We don't have beaches in Ohio, so the few times I got to go to a beach town, I tried to really soak it in.

As we got closer to the forest, I started to notice the flora more. There were huge trees, and beautiful flowers and bushes scattered along the Earth floor.

I could hear birds chirping as we walked along. It was a magnificent sight. Just like Violet's research had said, about ten minutes in we stumbled upon a trail with a sign that read *Lago Life*. "Right on point, Vi," I said as we began the hike.

"Well it's just looking at Google," Violet said, but I could tell she appreciated the compliment. Since the trail was actually in the forest, the plant life was bursting in our face. The trees in here were even taller than the ones surrounding the forest, and the floor was filled with bushes, flowers, and other small plants. It smelled like forest too, like a fresh garden blooming in the Spring. As before I could still hear the birds chirping away.

Violet looked terrified. I guess she wasn't into nature. "Vi, you good over there?" I asked.

"Not really, I didn't know that the forest was going to be like an actual forest," she replied.

I laughed.

"What did you think it was going to be?"

"I thought it was going to be more like our woods in America." I laughed a bit more.

Violet was by far one of the smartest people I know, but even she has her... dumber moments. Claire appeared to be biting back a laugh. I knew that if I made eye contact with her she would break, so I did. I looked her right in the eyes, and as expected, she burst out laughing. Apparently Violet did not appreciate my sense of humor as much as Claire because she was not even close to laughing.

"Sorry, we're just messing with you," I said, after I finished laughing.

When people you know are smart say something kinda dumb it's funny, because it doesn't happen very often, but when someone... not as smart, says something dumb it's not as funny because you expect it.

I guess I probably should have explained that to Violet. I forgot how sensitive she can be. I was about to start explaining that when she caught me by surprise. She genuinely smiled.

"It's okay," she said, still with a smile.

She even laughed at herself a bit. I was shocked, and she must have seen it on my face. "I've learned on this trip that it's okay to mess up, and that no one is perfect. It's okay to laugh at yourself when you do something funny," she explained.

I looked at Claire, still shocked, and she seemed to be feeling the same way as me. I looked back at Violet, and saw that she really meant it, and matched her smile. I was happy that this trip was helping her so much.

"Good for you, Vi," I said, a soft smile on my face.

She returned the smile, and Claire eventually joined us.

We continued on our hike, and like the first time, Violet's research came through and we arrived in twenty minutes. The lake was beautiful. Like Nico had said the water was crystal clear, and there was a tiny cliff to jump into the lake off of. It looked a bit high but was still safe. The vegetation was gorgeous, filled with flowers and trees.

We found a spot and set our stuff down where they would stay safe. I took off my clothes to reveal my swimsuit. Claire and Violet did the same. We were the only ones here, so we had the place all to ourselves. I trotted over to the water and dipped my toe in. The water was warm, like a giant bath. Pleased, I trotted back to Claire and Violet.

"How's the water?" Claire asked.

"Perfect," I replied. "It's like a giant bath."

"Nice, let's get in then," Claire said, walking towards the water.

"Wait, hold on. I think we should jump in," I said, stopping Claire. Claire turned around.

"From where?" she asked, suspicious. I pointed up at the hill.

"Where else?" I asked as if it was obvious. Violet's eyes went wide.

"Not again," Violet whined.

"Oh come on, this is nothing," I said.

I felt a sudden pang of slight guilt remembering Vegas, but this is what the trip is about. I know for a fact that Cassie would jump without hesitation. Then my mind flashed to that night in Vegas. Violet did say she would try for the rest of the trip. I loved Violet, but sometimes we have to push each other to make each other better.

"Do you remember Vegas?" I asked.

Something flickered in her eye. She knew what was coming next. "I do." She sighed.

"And do you remember when you said that you would live for the rest of the trip?" I asked her. She looked away. I could tell she was slightly embarrassed. I don't blame her.

"That was also about things built and designed like roller coasters. This is a beast of nature. It's a lot easier for something to go wrong. What if something happens?" she worried.

"What if it doesn't?" When I said it I looked her in the eyes.

I wanted her to face her fear, it's what Cassie would have wanted.

"What if it doesn't?" I repeated, this time more quiet, but loud enough to get the point across. Violet sat there and thought for a minute. Violet had an amazing brain, and I wouldn't be surprised if she found some statistics on this, or did the math to create them. I was expecting an argument to come out of her mouth, and was taken by surprise a bit.

"Okay," she finally agreed.

I was a bit shocked, that took way less convincing than I thought. "I said that I would live, so let's live."

I couldn't believe what just came out of her mouth.

"Well if she's doing it, it would look soft for me not to do it," Claire said, looking a bit surprised herself.

Violet smiled and playfully smacked her on the arm. "Well then let's go," I said cheerfully.

I could tell, as we walked up there, that Violet was still nervous. She was really facing her fear. Cassie loved her friends, and loved when they did things good for themselves. I could practically see her next to us smiling and trying to calm Violet down. She used to encourage all three of us when needed.

My mind flashed to a soccer meet about a year ago. I was so nervous, I was pacing the sideline before warm up. She jogged over to me and told me, "What's the worst that can happen?"

"I mess up," I obviously responded with.

"And what's so horrible about that?" she said, her warm smile never wandering from her face.

"What if I lose the game for us?" That grew her smile a little more.

"You need a whole team for that. You'll do great, Harls, and if you don't who cares? Aren't sports supposed to be fun?"

"I guess you're right," I said, a smile of my own appearing.

Most of those memories brought me pain and longing lately, but this one hurt slightly less. I wanted so badly to just have one more conversation with her, even if it was me saying goodbye. I wonder if I would have been able to if I knew she was going to die. I wondered if I could have prevented it somehow, maybe if I invited her over that night, or just called her and didn't hang up until morning. Or what if she just left her house just five minutes earlier or later, would that make a difference?

I shook my head. I had to stop. All I was doing was torturing myself.

I barely realized that we were at the top of the hill. I looked around, the hill was rock and the vegetation of the forest looked beautiful from up here. I looked down at the crystal clear water. I dug my toes into the rock, letting the smooth surface warm my feet. It was a gorgeous day, almost as if it were meant for us to do this. Claire and Violet were now both standing next to me, Claire on my left and Violet on my right.

"You guys ready for this?" I asked, my eyes locked forward.

"Let's do it," Violet said, her voice just a little shaky.

"Hell yeah," Claire responded.

I reached out my hand to Claire first. She took it. "For Cassie," I said, finally turning to look at her.

"For Cassie," she responded, never breaking the stare. I turned to Violet, offering my hand.

"For Cassie," she said, taking my hand in her own.

"On three?" They both nodded.

"Okay, one... Two... THREE," I shouted as we jumped.

As we jumped it felt as if time was in slow motion. Our hands were still interlocked, but our arms were above our head, straight up. I could hear Claire and Violet screaming next to me. As we fell, all of the memories I had with Cassie flashed through my mind at light speed. In an instant I could feel my body collide with the warm water, and I let go of my friends' hands. After I was submerged I shot back up to the surface. Claire and Violet shortly followed.

"Holy Hell!" Claire shouted.

"I can't believe we just did that!" She was still shouting. I smiled.

"I know!" Violet shouted back, a giant grin on her face.

"You guys ready for round two?" I asked giggling.

Violet splashed me. I started giggling again. They started laughing too. We splashed about and laughed in the warm water for almost two hours. We talked and raced each other swimming, and splashed about. The crystal clear water was practically shining as the sunlight reflected off of it. Finally we decided to dry off.

"Shoot! I forgot towels. Sorry, guys," Claire said, looking through the stuff, hoping to stumble upon a towel.

"It's okay, we can dry off up there," I said, pointing to the hill.

"Okay," she said, taking her hands out of her bag.

We began to walk back up there, and once we got to the top the ground was a bit hot. After adjusting to it, we laid our bodies on the rock surface and let the warm air and sunlight dry us as we talked.

"I still can't believe that we did that," Claire said as she looked at the sky. It was a beautiful day, and the sky was blue, not a cloud to be seen.

"I still can't believe that Violet did it," I teased.

"I can't believe that Harley hasn't made out with a random guy since Vegas," Violet responded quickly.

I smiled, then all three of us started laughing. As we lay there, basking in the sun, I couldn't help but think about Cassie. She would have been so happy with an experience like that. As soon as the thought appeared in my mind, the pain quickly followed. I tried to push it back again, but this time it was no use, so I let it go on, consuming my brain. My mind flashed to memories from years ago, each one bringing more sorrow than the last. I don't know how long later, but I felt someone shake me. I shook my head, trying to disconnect from the thoughts that lingered within. Claire was shaking me with worry painted across her face, and Violet was standing behind her looking just as concerned.

"Sorry, I was a bit zoned out," I stuttered, getting up.

"You scared us, we've been saying your name for like five minutes. Are you feeling okay?" Claire asked, helping me up.

"I'm good, just thinking." Claire looked at me, trying to see if I was lying.

"Are you sure?" she asked, her eyes drilling holes in me.

"I'm sure," I assured her.

She clearly didn't buy it, but she didn't push any further.

"We should start to head back," she said changing the subject.

"Yeah," I agreed.

Violet walked in front of us down the hill.

"I miss her too," Claire said just low enough to where I could barely hear.

Before I had a chance to respond, or even process what had just been said, she trotted to catch up with Violet. I stayed walking behind them as we walked down the hill. There was too much on my mind.

What's wrong with me? I couldn't help but wonder. Obviously my best friend died, but my mind can't even process simple things without somehow thinking of her. I felt like I was losing my mind trying to get my friend back.

We finally got back to the village, and decided to grab something quick for dinner. I barely ate it; I lost my appetite. My mind was swirling and it was starting to cause me a major headache. As soon as we got back to the hotel I changed into comfy clothes and crawled into bed. The bed felt so soft and comfy. I let myself lay there until I drifted away. I didn't get nightmares that night, just memories on repeat, each one haunting me just as much as a nightmare.

Claire

I'm fine is one of the most bullshit sayings there is. About ninety-eight percent of the time someone says they are fine, they are not actually "fine". As much as I love Harley she tends to do this a lot, and my sister used to do it even more than Harley.

Neither one of them thought that they could talk. Cassie had a great life, so she thought that talking about how she felt was complaining, which is unfair of her in her eyes. I loved my sister, but like any human being she was far from perfect, and had plenty of flaws.

Harley never opens up, or at least not to me and Violet. She did with Cassie, but now that she's gone, it's like a part of Harley has shut down. I just wish she would talk, but then again it is a bit unfair of me to ask that when I haven't been the best about it lately. I felt Harley stirring all night, I knew there was something wrong, and I would most likely have to pull it out of her.

My eyes fluttered open. There was a small stream of light showing through the curtains. Violet was sitting on a chair, her eyes glued to her laptop. She was most likely doing some type of school work. Harley was still asleep. As soon as we got back Harley had climbed into bed. I decided to join her.

I tapped her side.

"Morning, sunshine," I said. She groaned and rolled over. "Come on, we can get coffee once you wake up."

I felt like a mother bribing their child. "Fine," she grumbled.

She got up and went to the bathroom. I never woke up this early.

"So what are we doing today?" I asked as soon as she got back.

"Exploring the village."

"All right, let's get ready then," I said, getting up myself.

Once I finished using the bathroom it was Violet's turn. While we waited I looked outside. The bright sunshine had been replaced with gloomy clouds. It looked like there was about to be a giant storm.

"Hey, Harls, it looks like it's going to rain," I said turning back around.

"It doesn't matter. A little water never killed anyone," she responded, not looking towards the window.

I nodded, then turned back to the window. It looked like a bit more than just "a little water". I was about to argue, but then I realized that if it got bad we could always just come back to the hotel.

After Violet finally finished getting ready we set off. It was darker than normal outside because of the storm. The salty smell was strong today. I looked up at the sky, and just as earlier, the sky was filled with clouds that looked like they were about to drop some rain.

I shivered as a cold breeze cut by. I hated being cold. I was wearing jeans and a giant hoodie with a thermal underneath. Violet was wearing white jeans and a thick baby blue sweater, while Harley was somehow wearing dark jeans, and a tight-fitting black long sleeve that didn't look that thick.

As we kept walking I started to feel a slight drizzle. I put my hood on, like I said, I hated being cold. Cassie used to be the same way. Brandon almost always ended up giving her his jacket for the day.

Harley seemed unaffected by the rain. The more we walked the harder it rained. I could hear thunder clap and lightning strike in the distance. The trees began to sway with the wind. The rain began to pour down on us.

"Harley, I think we should just get some food for the day and bring it back to the hotel!" I shouted.

It was so loud from the weather that I had to shout.

"But we can explore the village, it should be fine!" she shouted back.

"Harley, we're in the middle of a storm!" I shouted, getting frustrated.

"We'll be fine!" she shouted.

I had enough. I was shocked that I had to argue this. We were in the middle of a storm for crying out loud.

"Harley, it's okay if we don't do anything today!" I assured her.

"What about Cassie?"

"Are you crazy? She wouldn't want to do this right now either."

"Please."

What was going on with her?

"What is wrong with you? What if it gets bad out here? We could end up like Cassie!" As soon as I said this a silence crept over us all.

I almost never lost my temper, but this time I couldn't stop it. I probably went too far this time. "I just want to make memories with you guys; you're all I have left," she almost whispered.

There was water running down her face, and some of it wasn't from the rain. I couldn't believe it, she was crying. I had never seen her cry before.

She stood in the rain before me, her long black hair was soaked and dripping water, and she stood with her arms crossed shivering as she cried. One of the strongest people I knew stood there, looking almost broken.

"You're all I have left," she repeated, this time even softer. A tear rolled down her cheek.

"Harl—"

"No!" she screamed, interupting me.

She looked angry now, as more tears spilled down her face.

"Almost every single person I ever loved left me. The one person that I knew for a fact would never do that to me was taken away from me. They were taken before I could even say goodbye! They were taken before we could even graduate from high school! Out of all of the people it had to be her in that car! It had to be my best friend that died!"

Tears were pouring out of her eyes now. "And the worst part is that there was nothing I could do to save her." She said it so softly.

She started sobbing. I rushed to hug her, crying myself. Violet joined us, also crying. I could feel the rain pounding down on us. All of the memories rushed back as I hugged my friend. "We will never leave you, Harls," Violet almost whispered.

"Someone or something would have to take me out to take me away, and as we know that is pretty hard to do," I said.

It made Harley laugh a bit, but it felt a little bitter sweet. I stepped away from Harley. She stood there, her T-shirt was now soaking wet and she was shivering like crazy. Her long black hair was now a mess from the wind.

"Come on, let's get some food and bring it back," I said.

"Okay?" I asked.

"Okay," she agreed.

She was slightly shaking.

"You look like shit by the way," I said as we started walking. She let out a slight laugh.

"Don't worry, you do too," she shot back, sending us both into a little laugh.

We were quiet the rest of the walk. We didn't need to talk about what just happened, we were just there. We were all thinking to ourselves, processing what had just happened in our own heads.

I couldn't help but still feel shocked. I had just seen someone who I never thought cried, cry. I thought about my sister. She never cried in front of people. I had seen her cry when she was young, but as she got older she stopped. I knew that she kept her emotions all inside, and if I could go back and do one thing, I would do a better job of being there for her. I thought that if I tried to get her to talk it would just push her away more.

That is one of my biggest regrets.

As we walked the rain decided to not let up and the wind howled, sending a chill down my back. I shivered the whole walk to get food and back to the hotel.

I hate nature.

On the walk back we were once again quiet, all in our own heads. Once we got to the hotel we took turns taking hot showers; me and Violet decided to let Harley go first due to the circumstances. I let Violet go next. As much as I hated being cold I wanted to make sure both of my friends were good first, especially after what just happened.

When it was my turn I practically ran to the shower. The water was hot, I let it run down my back sending warmth through my body. My toes started to burn, and for once I loved it. I closed my eyes as I washed my hair, letting the heat soak on my scalp.

After I got out, I blow dried my hair and threw on a giant hoodie and sweatpants and climbed into bed, and grabbed ice cream while I was at it. We each got a container at the store. Without saying anything I grabbed the remote and put on *Grown Ups*. It's one of our comfort movies.

I could feel myself begin to drift off into sleep. The bed was so warm and comforting, especially after that. I fell in and out of sleep for the next few hours. When I finally woke up, it was five o'clock. I rubbed my eyes and took a big morning stretch, well more like evening stretch. "Good morning." I turned to see Harley sitting up watching *Back to the Future*.

That was another one of our comfort movies. "Morning, is it still raining?" I asked, laying back down.

"I don't know, go check," she said.

"I can't, I'm too comfy," I complained.

"Please."

I remembered what had just happened so, as much as it pained me, I got up and looked out the window.

The rain was still there, but it had let up a lot. "It's drizzling," I said crawling back into bed. "Can we just stay here tonight?" I asked.

Harley smiled.

"Sure," she said, still smiling. I paused for a moment.

"I would give anything to give her back," I spat out.

Me and Harley had a no bullshit type of relationship. I may never be as close to her as my sister, but I will always be out front with her.

She looked at me, she understood. I wanted to comfort her, and in my opinion lies and BS don't help anyone.

"Trust me when I say I miss her too," I said again.

I turned my back and looked back out the window to make it easier.

"I hope you know that she would slap the shit out of you for not telling us sooner," I continued. I smiled for a second, I didn't have to look to know that Harley was too.

I turned back around. I walked over to Harley and took her hand into mine.

"Harley, I get that you don't have the best track record with people committing, but me and Violet will never ever leave you," I assured her.

"I second that," Violet said, sitting up lazily.

Harley looked at me, with a slight pain in her eye. I gave her hand a squeeze. "Thank you," she whispered.

Violet walked over and joined us. When we finally pulled away all of our eyes were red and watery. "I know that it wasn't on the bucket list, but Cassie did love a good movie night," I said.

Harley smiled.

"Sounds like a plan," she replied.

My sister, as much as she loved going out, loved a good movie night too. Just staying in with snacks and a good movie. I know we already watched a movie when we got back, but now we could at least be awake. After debating we all agreed on *The Sandlot*. We grabbed the snacks we bought and all sat down. It was nice, all three of us just watching a movie. I, once again, found myself missing my sister. I couldn't help it. I know that over time wounds heal, but they still leave a scar.

My sister will leave one hell of a scar.

After the movie we talked and laughed like we used to. There was still something off. We all knew it, the missing piece to the puzzle, but it was easier than the first time. It wasn't easy, but it was getting there. I fell asleep a little bit after the movie. That night my mind flashed to my sister's face. Her light brown hair, speckled with bits of gold and red. Her eyes, a beautiful amber, that would glisten in the sun. I missed her so much. No matter how much easier it got, I would always miss her.

Violet

Breakdowns happen, in machines, in animals, and in people. I've always been an emotional person; I feel no need to try and hide my feelings. It's what makes us human. Others try to be tough, and from a young age some are taught that crying is a weakness.

I believe that having the courage to cry in front of someone and show them what you're really feeling is brave. I love Harley to bits, but I just wished she would understand that. Harley always tries to be tough and make sure that everyone is having a good time, but you can only do that for so long before you... well, explode.

I slowly opened my eyes. It was the last day of our trip. I couldn't believe it. It felt so unreal. I sat up and looked around the room. As usual I was the first one up, but I let them sleep for about twenty minutes before I woke them up. In their defense, yesterday was a bit rough.

I walked over to the window and made sure it wasn't raining again. Thankfully the sun was out and shining. I walked over to Claire and gently nudged her.

"What time is it?" she groaned.

"8.24" I said softly.

She grumbled, pulling her pillow over her head. I smiled to myself, at least some things never change. Cassie and I were always the first ones up in the morning, and we practically had to drag Claire and Harley out of bed.

Claire was clearly not getting up, so I walked over to Harley.

"Harls, it's already 8.25," I said, gently poking her.

She grumbled something inaudible. I rolled my eyes. "Coffee," I said.

I didn't have to say any more.

I could almost feel Harley smirk. She slowly sat up and stretched. I smiled. I should have just started with that.

"Claire, coffee," Harley said sleepily.

Claire slowly sat up herself and took a big stretch. "I think you guys have an addiction," I said.

"Okay and what's the problem?" Harley said with a smile. I rolled my eyes at her.

"Whoa, I think you've been spending too much time with that one," Harley said, pointing at Claire.

"Hey," Claire said, throwing a pillow at Harley. Harley started laughing.

"Well, Violet, looks like you're going to be even more awesome then," Claire said, turning to me. I let out a giggle.

"So, what's the plan?" I asked, changing the subject. Harley grinned ear to ear.

"Well I thought we could start off by going down to the beach and just taking a walk."

I never thought I'd hear Harley want to take a walk. She must have seen the confusion written on my face.

"It was on the bucket list. She wanted to do it with Brandon, but I thought it could be fun for us too," she explained.

I nodded.

She continued on. "After that we can go get some lunch and then…" She paused for a moment. I raised an eyebrow. "And then we can go bungee jumping," she said, then sucked in a breath.

I was about to protest, but then remembered yesterday. At least the weather wasn't dangerous. I would most likely lose the argument anyway.

"Sounds good," Claire said, encouraging her. Harley went on.

"And then to end our trip I thought we could go to the beach at sunset, but still be back before it gets completely dark," she finished.

I nodded.

Claire did the same.

"Well let's start the end of our little adventure," Claire said, getting up.

After we finished getting ready and ate, and I delivered coffee as promised, we set off for the beach. The walk there was lovely. I could get used to the warm air, brushed with an occasional salty breeze. It was warm again today, without a cloud in sight.

It was kinda funny to me how that happens. Thankfully I had dressed right with a pastel blue T-shirt and a white pair of jean shorts. Claire had on a long sleeve in this weather, most likely scared it was going to be cold again. She hated the cold. Her black long sleeve had an ACDC oversized T-shirt over it, along with some jeans, and a pair of black converse. Harley wore a dark purple tank top and black jeans, and like Claire, black converse.

As we walked along, vendors lined the streets selling all types of goods, from food to hand-made objects. One of the vendors must have caught Harley's eye.

"Look, he has bracelets. I think we should get matching ones," she said. Claire and I smiled.

"I think that's a great idea," I said, walking towards the vendor.

Claire and Harley followed without a second thought.

The bracelets were the kind you tie around your wrist, and

they are supposed to stay there. We got the same kind in different colors. Mine was violet, duh, Claire's was pastel blue, and Harley's was a dark blue, like the swimsuits she got for us before the trip. After we bought them, we headed back towards the beach.

"Wait," I said, stopping. "We have to tie these on, and never take them off. That way Cassie can always be with us, along with each other."

I wanted to make sure that we had a piece of Cassie with us, and what better than a bracelet. Claire and Harley nodded, and began tying theirs on.

Once the bracelets were finally on, we began towards the beach once again. We finally got there a few minutes later. We walked along the beach, admiring the beautiful sight. The water was crystal clear, and I took off my shoes, so I could feel the warm sand between my toes.

"Can we sit down now? We've been walking for an eternity," Claire whined. Me and Harley shared a laugh as we sat down.

"Sorry about that, Claire," Harley said.

I covered my mouth with my hand, trying to fight a giggle.

"As long as we are not walking any more," Claire said, laying back. She propped herself up on her elbows.

"You know we still have to walk back," Harley said.

"Just enjoy the moment, I'll complain later," Claire said, holding a finger up at Harley.

Harley and I burst out into laughter. Claire shortly joined us. Once I recovered I looked at the beach. We were definitely not alone. There were a bunch of people milling about, surfacing, playing in the sand, and some walking like us moments ago.

I was starting to sweat from the warm air a little bit, but didn't care. I still wasn't used to the salty smell. I took a deep breath, letting it fill my lungs.

"You guys ready for bungee jumping?" Harley asked, snapping me out of my trance.

I had completely forgotten about that. Truth be told, I really did not want to do that, but something in me had changed a little bit. I was terrified, but I made a promise, I would let go just for the span of this vacation, it kind of sucked, but it meant something.

"Hell yeah," I said softly.

Harley looked at me like she had just seen a ghost. Claire looked equally as shocked.

"I want to be able to say I lived someday, even if it was just for twelve days," I said with a shrug. Harley smiled, while Claire still looked a little shocked.

"Maybe I'm rubbing off on you," Harley said with a chuckle. I smiled.

"I'm still terrified, but I'll give it a go," I admitted.

Harley smiled and put her hand on my shoulder. I smiled back. Claire still looked utterly confused.

"All right, I guess I look like a giant pansy if I don't go, so I am definitely in," Claire finally said. Harley burst out laughing. I swatted her on the arm, slightly giggling. When Harley finally stopped laughing she checked her phone.

"We should probably get going," she said, getting up.

Claire and I got up with her, and began the walk back to the hotel. I looked back at the beach as we walked away, in disbelief that this was our last day of the trip. So much had happened in so little time, I felt almost like a different person.

As we walked I made sure that every sight we saw was carved in my memory. I wanted to remember this trip, even the tough parts.

I think that the tough parts are the most important, because that's what makes you appreciate the good ones.

When we got back to the hotel we got a transport for the first time this trip and set off to "fun".

"Thank God! I am so sick of walking," Claire said, climbing into the transport.

Harley rolled her eyes, and followed Claire into the transport.

"You know we technically could have walked, but it would have taken us like forty minutes," Harley said, smirking.

"If you told me that we were going to walk for forty minutes I would have stayed at the hotel," Claire said.

Harley shot her a grin.

"That's why I got a transport," she pointed out.

Claire couldn't help but smile, even through her eye roll.

"Besides, if I did decide to have us walk, I just wouldn't tell you until we were about twenty-five minutes in," Harley said, still smirking.

"You suck," Claire said, with a laugh.

"And you're lazy," Harley shot back, grinning.

I looked out the window as we drove. The city was beautiful as we drove. As we drove by the beach, the light reflected off of the clear water beautifully creating a shimmer in the ocean, and the sand looked warm and inviting. How I wish I was there instead of jumping off of a ledge at a great height. The nerves were finally starting to hit me. Suddenly the car seemed like it was going one hundred miles an hour.

I felt sick.

"Vi, you okay?" Harley asked. I nodded.

My mouth felt dry and I started to sweat. "Are you sure?" Claire asked.

It was hard to lie to Harley, but impossible to lie to Claire, especially when she's my best friend. I nodded again. Claire looked like she didn't buy it, but held her tongue. She sat back, looking over at me every few minutes, with concern written all over her face. I felt horrible for worrying my friend, and started to regret saying yes to this.

What was I thinking? Stupid, stupid girl. I have no idea what had gotten into me, I didn't even ask for the name of the place so I could at least research it to make sure it's safe. They could have fifty accidents a day for all we know.

A million different scenarios played through my head of something going wrong. Why did I agree to be carefree? Maybe I thought I was Cassie for a minute. I don't know how that girl was so fearless, her and Harley both. They both definitely had their issues, but courage was for sure not one of them.

I looked down at my hands and realized that they were shaking. I wondered if there was any color left in my face.

"We're almost there," the driver said, from up front.

"Thank you," all three of us responded at the same time.

If I wasn't about to throw up all over the transport I would have laughed at our in sync response. I barely felt when Claire lightly grabbed my hand.

"You don't have to do this, Vi," Claire whispered to me. She looked like a worried mother.

"I know, but I'm going to," I responded without a thought.

Stupid. I don't know why I did that. In fact I was quite mad at myself for not thinking, usually I was amazing at thinking things through, it's my thing. I don't know what's gotten into me. Claire literally gave me an out and I wasted it for what? Pride? Self assurance? I wanted to kick myself. "Okay, if you want to, I just wanted to make sure you didn't feel like you had to," Claire said, removing her hand.

I just nodded, I couldn't speak.

Shortly after my idiocy, the transport slowed to a stop. I stepped out to find a trail pointing to a path. I gulped, in hopes I would swallow my fear. My legs were unstable under me, shaking with every step along the path towards our doom. Claire and Harley both looked perfectly fine. Claire did look a tad nervous, but nothing compared to me.

They were having a normal conversation, as if we weren't about to do a death-defying jump, that might not defy death if one little thing goes wrong. My breathing got heavier and heavier until I was practically panting.

"Guys," I said lightly, stopping.

I needed a minute to catch my breath and clear my mind. I felt worse than on the roller coaster. Harley and Claire turned around and rushed over to me.

"Vi, are you okay?" Claire asked.

"Hey, you don't have to do this, it's a lot to ask," Harley assured me.

Something surged in me right before I opened my mouth. I remembered why I said yes in the first place. I wanted to live; I wanted to be able to say I looked fear in the eye and told it to screw off.

"I can do this. I just need to catch my breath for a minute," I assured them.

"Are you sure?" Claire asked.

This it, my last out, I could just say no and never have to jump. "I'm sure," I said.

"Okay, we'll give you a minute," Harley said, taking a step back.

I started to gain control of my breathing, slowly reeling it back in until it was a normal pace.

I can do this.

I stood up straight and lifted my chin. I was not going to let fear control me. I tried to channel my old friend, the one who didn't even have fear in her vocabulary. Cassie would love to do this, hell it was on her bucket list.

"I'm good," I said, walking towards Harley and Claire.

Claire still looked deeply concerned, like I might crumble any second. "One hundred percent?" Claire asked.

"One thousand," I said confidently, even if I didn't feel it. Harley clapped her hand on my back.

"That's what I'm talking about, kid," she said, slightly sounding like a dad.

I winced at the thought, then brushed it off. My dad used to always say that to me. He would want me to be brave too. He would want me to go and live my life. I remember his last sentence, *Don't ever forget how much I love you, kid, you make me proud every day. Live everyday like it's your last.*

As we walked I thought about the people I had lost, the scars deep in my heart. I hoped that they were watching this. I wanted to do this for them as much as myself, if not more. With every step up the trail I felt a little stronger, like both of them were here with me. *I can do this.* I repeated it to myself over and over again until it was carved into my brain.

When we finally got to the platform my heart was beating out of my chest. It was a platform overlooking a giant cliff. If there wasn't the possibility I was about to die I would have admired the view.

From here you could see the luscious trees and in the far background the ocean. It was a beautiful sight. I tried so desperately to swallow back the intense nerves, but my hands were visibly shaking.

A worker took us to the jump site and discussed payment with Harley while me and Claire sat back. Claire took my shaking hand and placed it in hers.

"Vi, you don't have to do this, it's not like a roller coaster," Claire said.

I looked into her eyes, I saw concern in between the brown and green swirl of the hazel. "Do you remember the promise we made in the airport?" I asked.

It felt like so long ago, and not twelve days. She nodded. "I meant it when I promised," I said.

I looked into her eyes once again, and found understanding.

"You two coming?" Harley complained.

I smiled while Claire rolled her eyes.

"Just for that eye roll you're going first," Harley said, pointing at Claire.

"Least I'll be able to say I did it before you," Claire said over her shoulder as she walked by Harley.

Harley just rolled her eyes.

"Fine, I'll do it first," Harley said, stepping next to Claire.

"Not the first time you did something first," Claire snorted.

"Claire." I gasped.

Harley started laughing.

"Was that a slut shame?" Harley asked, laughing.

"Maybe it was," Claire teased.

Harley just shrugged and smiled. "How's Alex?" Harley asked, smirking. Claire's face went ruby red.

Alex was a guy we had once walked in on Claire making out with. We have not let her live it down.

"You ladies ready?" a voice said from behind us. I turned to see a worker walking over.

She had long black hair and beautiful dark skin. "Yes we are," Harley responded for all of us.

"You have an amazing English accent," I noticed out loud.

I learned Spanish along with other languages at a young age, and often second language accents are difficult to master.

"I'm from America," the girl said.

"That makes more sense," I said, feeling slightly stupid. She giggled a little.

"Don't worry, my Spanish accent is horrible," she said. I smiled sheepishly.

"So who's first?" she asked, turning her attention to Harley and Claire.

"I can go first," Harley volunteered.

"Perfect, let's get you harnessed up," the lady said walking towards the harness area.

She looked young, not much older than myself.

"How long you've been doing this?" Harley asked, as she harnessed her up.

"A few months now, I just graduated last year and decided to take a gap year between then and my first year of college so I can refresh," she said. "I'm Bell by the way."

"That's so awesome," Harley cooed as she got strapped up. "I'm Harley, and the grumpy one is Claire, and blondie is Violet," Harley said, nodding her head towards us.

"Well, are you ready to jump, Harley?" Bell asked.

"Hell yeah," Harley responded without an ounce of fear.

I could never understand how she was always so brave, it was something I deeply envied. Harley walked over to the jump site and got hooked up to the bungee cord.

"All right," Bell said, stepping back. "You can jump

whenever you're ready." Harley looked at us so her back was to the jump site.

She did a quick salute and jumped backward without hesitation.

Crazy bitch, I thought to myself as she fell.

We watched as the cord caught her and she began to bounce to the cord until she was dangling there. Bell and another worker reeled her back up to the jump site.

"There's a waiting area on the platform right below us so you can see your friends jump," Bell said, unstrapping Harley from the harness.

"All right, thanks," Harley said. Then she looked at me and Claire.

"Guys, it is so awesome, and you can say you lived after," Harley said.

It might have been my imagination, but it appeared she even winked at me. I watched as she walked down the stairs, down to the next platform to watch us.

"Who's next?" Bell asked. She smiled sweetly.

"I can go," Claire said, stepping forward.

"Okay," Bell said, leading her towards the harnesses.

The nerves started to build up even more as I watched Claire get strapped up. She seemed slightly more nervous than Harley, but nothing like me.

I was a mess.

Once again I watched a friend jump off of a platform to be saved by a bouncy rope. When they reeled Claire up she was smiling ear to ear. After they got her unharnessed she walked over to me. She looked at me, then gave me a hug. I prayed that she couldn't feel my shaking.

"You can do this," she assured me.

I just nodded, my mouth was so dry I didn't think it was possible for any words to form, let alone come out. She gave me one last tight squeeze and then let go. I watched her disappear down the stairs.

"You ready?" I heard a sweet voice ask. I looked up to see Bell smiling.

"It's okay to be nervous, sometimes we get grown men crying," she assured me. I forced out a smile.

I could feel the nerves in my body buzzing. I took a shaky step towards the harness, and then another, until I was walking there. As they harnessed me up all I could hear was the ringing in my ears, and the drumming in my chest. *I can do this*, I told myself as I tried to slow my breathing.

I thought of Cassie, how she would practically be jumping up and down, excited to jump. I thought of my dad next, how he would be smiling calmly, he would tell me fear is a state of mind. I smiled at the thought.

"Okay you're good to go," Bell said.

She directed me towards the jump site and hooked me up to the bungee cord. "You are all hooked up; you can jump whenever you're ready," she said.

*F*ear *is a state of mind.*

I repeated it in my head once more for good measure, picturing my dad saying it to me. I looked down over the towering jump site. I allowed myself to find comfort in memories of my old friend and my father. Without thinking I closed my eyes and jumped.

When I opened my eyes I felt weightless, like I was flying. A scream escaped my mouth as I plummeted towards the Earth. I didn't hear much of it through the sound of blood rushing past my ears. My life flashed before my eyes, bringing back memories I thought long forgotten.

I barely noticed the amazing view. All in an instant I felt the rope catch me and catapult me back up, and then again and again, each time weaker than the last until I was there, dangling in the wind.

When my feet were finally back on the platform I was shaking. I was still in disbelief that I had actually done that. I barely heard Bell when she told me where my friends were. I walked down the stairs to where my friends were waiting for me.

"Vi you did it!" Harley squealed. Claire gave me a huge smile.

"We're proud of you, Vi!" Claire said.

I didn't even notice that I was smiling. I started to gather my thoughts.

I just did that.

I felt strong, like I could take on anything, and the best part was, I had a bit of fun doing it. "I'm not doing it again though," I finally responded.

Violet and Harley shared a laugh. Some fun things are best not repeated. "I guess I can say that I lived now." I beamed.

Harley matched my smile.

"Hell yeah you can," she said, throwing her arm around my shoulders.

The sky was a beautiful mix of orange and pink. I closed my eyes and breathed in the salty breeze as it swept my hair back. I looked up again at the sunset. Claire was sitting to my left, with Harley on hers. It was about 6.40, and we were sitting on the beach watching the sunset. It was the last activity before we went home. I couldn't believe that it was over. So much had happened on this trip, yet I still craved more. More time with my friends, more time to laugh and enjoy life, but I guess we all end up wanting that. I'm sure Cassie would have loved to have more time.

"I can't believe it's over," Claire said, almost reading my mind.

"Me too," I agreed.

"It's never over," Harley said. Claire and I turned to look at her.

"We don't need to be on vacation to make the most out of every day." She paused for a second, letting her words really sink in. "From this moment on, I promise to try to make the best out of each and every day of my life, because that's what Cassie did, and would keep doing given the chance."

"Me too," I said.

"Make that three," Claire said, putting out her pinky finger.

We put them together, creating an unbreakable promise. I turned my attention back to the beach, and took my last breaths of the salty air.

Harley

I awoke to the sound of my alarm. I rubbed my eyes as I sat up. It was the first time this trip that Violet didn't have to wake me or Claire up. After a stretch, I got up and turned the alarm off. I walked over to the window and looked out of it one last time. It all started to hit me.

This trip was done. We had lived. It made me miss Cassie more, but in a way it helped me say goodbye. I looked down at the bracelet we got, and rubbed it. So much had happened in such a short amount of time. I turned around to see Violet up and moving, and Claire lazily and slowly getting out of bed.

"Let's go home," Violet said, picking out her outfit. I smiled.

"Let's go home," I agreed softly.

I walked over to my suitcase and picked out my outfit. It was just black leggings with a hoodie and a tank top underneath since we were going to have a long flight. Claire had on gray sweatpants with a giant jacket, and Violet had on a white sweater and black leggings like me. "You guys ready?" Claire asked.

"Yep," I said, walking over to her and Violet.

"All right, then let's go home," she said opening the door.

Violet followed her out. I walked out the door, then looked back at the now empty room. I turned back around and shut the door behind me.

Violet

Walking into the airport felt unreal. Everything that happened throughout this trip flashed through my mind. I felt like a different person entirely. I thought of my friend, the friend who lived everyday like it was her last, and made an adventure out of an ordinary day.

I wondered what her regrets were when she died. We all have regrets, but I never knew hers. Can someone like her even have regrets? I know I certainly do, but I guess that regrets are a part of life. There will always be a path we didn't choose, but how do we know that that would have worked out better? We never choose it. The other option might have been ten times worse, but I guess we'll never know.

I have regrets, many of them. From not taking a chance to making a fool of myself for not thinking, but I know that when I was on this trip I didn't have any. I choose to live for twelve days, and for the rest of my life I can say those twelve days were regret free.

I miss Cassie and I always will, but if I learned anything from being her friend, I want to live my life like she lived hers, without regrets.

I want to live.

"Vi, our boarding group was called," Harley said, getting up.

"Okay," I said, also getting up.

As I walked towards the jet bridge, I promised myself that I would do everything to make sure I don't have any regrets someday.

Claire

This is it, I thought as I walked on the jet bridge. Just like that the trip was over. I thought of my sister, and what it would have been like if she was there. How things would be different. I would get to meet my future nieces and nephews, and make fun of her when we got old. A part of me pretended that I was flying home to her right now, that she would be waiting at the airport for us. I know that it's going to be a long time before we reunite, but in a way I felt like she was still with me. A part of her will always be with me, no matter how small.

This trip helped me feel connected to her in a way, as if she was sitting right next to me. I could almost hear her laugh and smell her citrus perfume. I don't know what my life has in store for me, but I know that no matter what I do my sister will always be with me, watching down. I want to make her proud more than anything.

I went on my phone and started looking through all of the photos and videos of us. I found one of us when we were seven and putting on a "concert" for our parents. I smiled as a tear rolled down my cheek.

Before I came on this trip I didn't go out of my comfort zone a lot, I was just… there, but something in me changed in the past twelve days. I now understand why Cassie did so many crazy things, because she learned and grew every step of the way. She always knew who she was, and now I want to do that for myself, but even more for my sister. She may have died, but her memory never will. The memory of her is something I will treasure forever. It still hurts, but it reminds me to be strong and to keep fighting, and to go outside my comfort zone, because that's what she would do.

Harley

I looked out the window as our flight took off, and watched as the airport faded as we got further and further away. Whenever I pictured bungee jumping or clubbing or going to spring training, I pictured doing it with my best friend. Who else are you supposed to do crazy things with if not your best friend?

Going through life without your best friend kind of sucks, but I feel that I finally got to say goodbye in some weird way. I'll never forget my best friend, how could anyone forget such an amazing person? It still hurts to think about her, and it will forever. It hurts to know that you'll never get to be with such an amazing person on this Earth again, but everyday it hurts just a little less. Like I said it will always hurt, but maybe someday I'll be able to think of her without wanting to scream or kick something.

Like the rest of the human body, when someone leaves a mark or tears a piece out of a heart it heals, but it always leaves a scar, but the biggest scars always have the best stories. I started to drift asleep on the plane, and I didn't have any nightmares. I was able to dream of my friend, and for once I was able to smile at the memories.

Epilogue

Cassie, March 2, 2021

I looked out of the window. It was pitch dark except for the light coming from the car. "Cas, you coming?" Brandon asked.

"Yeah," I said, getting out of the car.

We were parked on a hill. I shut my door and walked over to Brandon. I looked at where the electrical box was. The car was positioned perfectly. Me and Brandon grabbed our bags and put them on the other side of the hill then walked back to the car.

"Ready?" I turned to look Brandon in the eyes. My blood pounded with adrenaline.

"Ready," I responded.

We pushed the car down the hill and then sprinted to take cover on the other side. We made it just in time to duck. I heard the explosion on the other side, and could feel the heat.

"You okay?" Brandon asked.

"Yeah, you?"

"Perfect," he replied.

I nodded and stood up. I threw my bag over my shoulder.

"Cassie, wait," Brandon said, grabbing my wrist as I started to walk off.

I turned to him. He looked handsome as ever. His floppy brown hair and hazel eyes. "Are you sure you want to do this?" he asked.

I looked into his eyes. I gave him a quick kiss.

"I'm sure," I promised him.

I smirked as I walked away. He quickly caught up. "That was crazy," he said smiling.

I matched his smile.

"Well life is for the living after all," I replied.

We walked off towards the start of our adventure without looking back.